Black Tide

ISBN:1-58961-414-3

Published by
PageFree Publishing, Inc.
109 South Farmer Street
Otsego, MI 49078
(269) 692-3926 (269) 92-3651 Fax
www.pagefreepublishing.com

Black Tide

by

Ingrid McLaughlin Taylor

To Amanda,
"my "foo-foo" girl"
Thank you for your
un-ending support
XO Ingrid :)

Dedication

To Christa Charlotte McLaughlin, also known as "Mom", whose unrelenting belief that I can be a success at anything I try, makes me keep trying harder.

To Charles "Chuck" Joseph Taylor, III, whose love and support has given me the freedom to pursue my dreams.

Acknowledgements

I am one of the luckiest women in the world. My life is filled with loved ones, many of whom are willing to wear different hats, as needed. In order of appearance, I want to thank Christa McLaughlin and Carol Cleveland, my very first "gentle readers."

Heartfelt thanks to my terrific friends from my writers' group at Bass Pro Shops' corporate offices in Springfield, Missouri; Angela Filbeck, Constance Whiston, Tammy Plemmons, Deborah Bedell, and Christina Reed. An extra special thank you goes to my awesome editor and friend, Angela Filbeck, for her time and continued encouragement. Thank you, Ann Crellar, a peach of a proofreader. Kudos to Christina Reed, for her artistic contributions.

Finally, thank you to my sweetheart of a husband, Chuck Taylor. You are the greatest.

Chapter One

The sky blackened in a matter of minutes. From out of nowhere thick, angry clouds rolled in and smothered what was left of the daylight. Mikela shuddered and turned on the SUV's headlights, glad that she had purchased such a heavy vehicle to make this journey. A few seconds later, big splats of water blurred her vision as the *nor'easter* broke loose over the mainland.

In the intensity of the storm, Mikela pulled to the side of the deserted road and decided to wait it out under the dense canopy of thick pines standing like sentinels along this lonely stretch of pavement. With the motor running and the defroster at full blast, she debated whether to leave the radio on. The sound of the announcer's voice was the only human contact she'd had since last filling her gas tank.

Continuing on her journey was out of the question. As the static took control of the lone voice on the radio, it left her with nothing but her own thoughts, giving her time to reflect on her life. Her only claim to fame was that she'd made it to her mid-thirties without a moment's boredom. Instead of marrying and having a family as most of her friends had done, she had traveled the world as a corporate courier. She was never anywhere long enough to form lasting relationships. The death of her parents six months earlier had come as a shock, making her realize she was alone in the world. She felt the need for roots. Now here she was, thirty-six, on her way to claim her inheritance—a dilapidated old lighthouse off the northern coast of Maine, bought by her parents in the seventies as an investment for their old age. She vaguely remembered the old structure. It wasn't a working lighthouse, even then. They'd all spent a pleasant enough week picnicking on the beach, splashing around in the cold, salty waves, and sleeping on cots at night. '*Papa, mama and baby bear*' was how they had referred to themselves at the lighthouse more than a decade earlier—such sweet memories.

Thunder cracked over her head while lightning jagged across the sky. The radio announcer's voice was lost once again as reception became impossible, and then it went dead. Her nerves were on edge and she wasn't certain whether it was from the static electricity in the air or the sense of total isolation she felt. The last town was more than an hour behind her and ahead lay only the isolated island community of Beam and the uncertain bridge over which she had to cross.

Mikela caught a glimpse of far-off headlights in the rear view mirror. She checked the vanity mirror to see if she looked as frazzled as she felt. Long drives always made her feel rough. The dim interior light showed her intense dark brown eyes. Eyes that looked a bit like road maps from the strain of driving in bad weather. Her auburn hair was tousled by the wind at the last stop for gas. Absentmindedly, she raked her fingers through the curls, but the gesture did nothing to tame the mass of hair that circled her head like a mane. She sighed. She loved adventures but her current mood, coupled with what might be a deadly storm, made her pray for safety.

The radio announcer's voice suddenly broke through the static and wind battering against her vehicle.

"All roads are closed until further notice. The highway patrol is urging all motorists to get off the road and find shelter immediately. I repeat: all roads in our listening area are closed. The Beam Island Causeway is flooded. There is no traffic on or off of the island except for emergency vehicles. Stay tuned for further updates."

Mikela heard, as well as felt, a rumbling thud nearby and turned in her seat to see an old oak tree topple through the pines from the force of the storm. The gale force winds were beating mercilessly against her vehicle. Pieces of live tree limbs and branches were slamming against the windows, along with dead wood and other bits of debris. White-knuckled from her death grip on the steering wheel, she wondered what her next move should be. Should she leave the shelter of the trees where one might fall and crush her at any moment or should she venture toward the causeway where there was no protection from the wind and water?

She squeezed her eyes shut. She was alone and frightened and didn't know what to do. The static on the radio came and went. She'd never felt so alone. A monstrous gust of wind rocked the SUV and Mikela's heart slammed in her chest. *She was going to be killed!*

"Hey!" A loud thud and then another. "You alright?" She thought she heard a muffled shout above the wail of the wind. Fearful of what she would see, she turned slowly to look out her side window. A gloved fist was banging on the glass near her head. She met the glare of two dark eyes staring out from a yellow hooded face. She gasped, startled out of her fear.

"Yes! Yes!" Mikela rolled down the window and immediately the wind whipped into her full force, taking her breath away. "Oh, thank God!"

"Don't try to talk. Follow me." The figure clad in yellow raingear shouted brief instructions. "Stay close. We're only a quarter mile from the turn off. Follow my tail lights."

"Okay, yes!" Mikela cried in relief, tears streaming down her face. "I'll be right behind you! Thank you! Thank you!" Mikela silently thanked God and this stranger over and over. Her nerves were stretched to the limit. She was so sure she'd be crushed in the unrelenting fury of the storm that she couldn't stop the flow of grateful tears. *At least if she was killed now, someone would know. She wouldn't die alone.*

She closed the window and shifted her SUV into *drive*. Mikela realized that in her fear she'd closed her eyes and hadn't seen the truck drive up behind her. Now she watched in the rear view mirror as headlights backed away a few feet, then swerved around her, followed by the eerie red glow of the taillights from the big pick-up truck that now pulled in front of her. The driving rain still made it hard to see clearly. Her tears didn't help, either. She wiped at her eyes, still trembling, but determined to follow this stranger to safety. *She wasn't out of the woods yet!* She pressed her foot lightly on the accelerator, barely giving it any gas, as the wind and water tried to wrench the steering wheel out of her hands. She couldn't stop trembling, but kept her eyes glued to the tail lights in front of her. It seemed like hours before the truck started to make a right hand turn. A wide, muddy path snaked through the dense pines and white birch trees into the heart of a forest. The road wasn't paved and the SUV leaned first right and then left as it worked its way through potholes and high spots, but the danger of toppling over was gone, thanks to the thick wall of trees that provided some protection from the storm. Rain still made the taillights ahead of her appear blurry and Mikela almost ran into the back of the truck when she realized it had come to a full stop, probably a mile or more into the woods.

The glowing red taillights went out and Mikela could see that the truck was a big, dark Ford. It had a camper on the back and she faced its entry door. She turned off the engine with a loud sigh of relief. The camper stood directly in her line of vision as her eyes strained to search through the pelting rain for a house or structure of some kind. Trees were all she could make out.

The figure in the yellow slicker came around the side of the camper and stood at her window. She still could only see two dark eyes. She rolled the window down to speak.

"Thank you so much, you saved my life!" gushed Mikela.

"Where's your gear?" shouted the deep, masculine voice coming from inside the raingear.

"I have a duffel bag in the back." Mikela pressed a button on the console that would unlock the rear hatch. The stranger moved away and Mikela closed her window, removed her keys and put them in her handbag. She grabbed her umbrella, unlatching her seatbelt as she slid out of the truck. She landed with both loafer-clad feet in a deep, cold puddle, grimacing as the icy water sent shivers down her spine. She managed to lock the SUV but lost the battle to open her umbrella in the blustering wind and rain. She heard the rear door of the SUV slam shut and her mysterious helper came around the back of her car, carrying her bulging duffel bag.

"Follow me."

Mikela tried to shake the mass of hair out of her eyes as the wind played with her locks. She kept her head down and followed the yellow legs in front of her, sloshing through mud and stepping over broken limbs and rocks along the pathway. When she looked up to see where she was heading, it looked like they were climbing into a tree house. She counted six wooden stairs as they stepped off the ground. Two huge old oak trees stood on either side of the steps. Under the shelter of the eaves, the figure in front of her unlatched a screened door and held it open for Mikela as he pushed a massive carved oak panel inward. She stepped into a large shadowy room, dim light filtering down from the ceiling. The skylights barely illuminated the hulk of a huge, free-standing, stone fireplace in the center of the room, its welcoming fire casting shadows on the walls. The inviting warmth enveloped her as she stepped further inside. The wailing of the wind became muffled and then ceased as the door closed solidly behind her.

Two beautiful dogs came bounding from behind the fireplace and sniffed at Mikela's ankles, tails held high, alert for danger from the unfamiliar woman who entered their home.

"Oh, they're beautiful!" Mikela cried. "What breed are they?" Her handbag dropped to the floor as she ruffled the long, soft fur on the dogs' necks.

Mikela could only see the broad back of her tall rescuer as he pulled the dripping yellow rain slicker over his head and hung it on a peg. The slicker caught on his red flannel work shirt and as he turned toward her, she glimpsed a muscular and solid belly, a dusting of dark hair. He pulled on his shirt with one hand while running the other through his jet-black hair. She looked into serious, deep set brown eyes and felt herself becoming self-conscious under his intent gaze.

"Their father is wolf and the mother is husky. Malamute. Abby and Niska, say hello to…?"

"Oh. Mikela. Mikela Williams." Mikela turned and thrust out her hand to the tall, handsome stranger and flashed her brightest smile. "I really thought I was a 'goner' out there. Thank you so much for helping me."

"You're quite welcome, Mikela Williams. What are you doing on the road in this weather? We don't get many tourists during hurricane season." She looked up into smoldering deep, dark eyes.

"Oh, I'm no tourist," Mikela unzipped her jacket and shrugged out of it. The smaller of the dogs took the jacket from Mikela and brought it to her master. Mikela laughed aloud, "Your dogs are wonderful. Did you train them yourself?"

"Yes, they were four days-old when I got them. I had to bottle feed them, so I'm their mom and dad. Abby and Niska are my family." He hung up Mikela's jacket on the peg next to his own. "Let's have a hot drink and you can tell me what brought you here."

"I think some hot coffee would do the trick. Can I help?" She followed the broad shoulders to a room whose windows looked into a forest. "This is such a wonderful house," Mikela smiled as they entered the room. She felt so safe in this wooden structure, nestled in the woods. The inside of the kitchen was very simple. A refrigerator on her left, lots of counter space and handmade cabinets. A gas cook stove was on the far wall flanked on either side by small appliances. Plants hung on either side of the window located over the sink with a view that looked into the scenic forest beyond and a log cabin-style shed at the end of a stone walkway. A small, square oak table with four mis-matched wooden chairs sat to the right side of the room, surrounded by uncurtained windows. Dog bowls were sitting on plastic placemats by the back door.

Her rescuer opened a cabinet door and took out two mugs. "Here. You can put water in the coffee pot. There's milk in the fridge if you need it. Sugar's on the table. Spoons are in here," he nodded as he pulled out a drawer for her. "How about something to eat? I've got cold cuts in the fridge or there's some venison stew I could warm up." He turned to watch Mikela filling the coffee pot at the sink and smiled. He caught himself wondering if his mysterious guest would welcome the self-imposed isolation he had chosen for himself.

Mikela poured water into the top of the coffeemaker and slid the cover back on. She watched as the steaming brown liquid filled up the pot. Standing at the counter next to this handsome man, Mikela was completely at ease, adding milk and sugar to her mug, acting as if she'd lived there all her life! He picked up the coffee pot and filled both mugs. Guiding her with his free hand lightly on her elbow, he directed her toward the kitchen table. The beautiful dogs circled a time or two, and then lay down on a huge cushion in a corner behind the table, eyes and ears ever watchful, ever alert. Mikela sat with elbows on the table, cradling her mug in both hands and took a long drink. She could feel the heat of the coffee warm her from the inside out as she swallowed. It felt so good to be warm again.

"Now, Mikela Williams, tell me your story." Dark, intelligent eyes sparkled with interest as he leaned toward her. She noticed that he had deeply etched dimples, his face a canvas of his life, a bit weathered with a scar on his right cheek, making him all the more rugged looking. She was caught up in those eyes, her heart beating as she felt the pull of attraction toward this stranger. She gave herself a mental pinch to straighten up. She did not know this man and he might be expecting a big reward for saving her from the storm! She sat up in her chair and began her brief story.

"Well, there's not much to tell. I've inherited a lighthouse and I'm going to move into it, fix it up for my home and put down some roots. I've traveled all of my adult life and now I'm ready to settle down. It's the lighthouse on the north side of Beam Island. Have you seen it?" Mikela took another long sip of her coffee and enjoyed its warmth again.

"Yes…I have," the stranger slowly replied. "What do you know about the lighthouse? I think you may be making a mistake moving there."

"Well, nothing really." Mikela was a bit put off by his lack of enthusiasm. "Tell me about its history, it sounds very intriguing. I could use a good adventure!" She smiled brightly, hoping for a similar response, but he dropped his head and fidgeted with his mug.

"The lighthouse was erected in 1869. You'll notice it's in a very isolated location. Its purpose wasn't to warn ships of the shallow waters, but rather to alert the few islanders that a ship had gone down. During the Civil War, an outlaw band from the mainland had killed the peaceful native tribe that lived there during the summer months. A few of the women were spared to become the slaves of the marauder band that built the lighthouse—probably a fate much worse than death. Each time a ship went down, the wreckage and bodies would be looted. The bodies from the native people as well as the bodies of the shipwrecked passengers were dragged to the edges of the cliffs and thrown over. There are caves under that side of the island where human bones and pieces of the ships can still be found. At night, it's said you can hear the cries of the native women, mourning the loss of their men and children." He stopped speaking and looked directly into Mikela's startled eyes. "I don't mean to frighten you or spoil your plans, but you can't stay at the lighthouse, Mikela Williams."

"Well, I—I'm not sure what to say, but I certainly can't change my plans. I have nowhere else to go. My parents left me this lighthouse and I owe it to their memory to use it as they intended. I certainly won't be waiting for ships to crash into it!" She swallowed the last of her coffee and noticed that the wind outside had intensified in the last few minutes and was very aware of her precarious situation. Suddenly this stranger was not the warm and comforting presence that she'd felt earlier. Her rescuer looked very serious as he got up from the table and walked to the counter to retrieve the coffeepot. He picked it up and refilled both of their mugs.

"You need to look at the situation very carefully. Many bad things have happened out at the lighthouse. Some think that descendants of the original outlaws live in the underground caves that crisscross the island. You're a woman on your own. You have no protection. Do you even own a gun?" He took a quart of milk from the fridge and brought the sugar bowl and a spoon to the table.

Mikela looked up at him wondering if he wasn't another male chauvinist, thinking of every woman as a hapless creature if she didn't have a man in her life.

"I really do appreciate your concern. You've been very kind to me and I'm sure you mean well, but there's really nothing I can do. I simply can't change my plans. I need to see this through. I'm not a stupid person and I will be careful. I really don't think a weapon is necessary." The longer she considered that he might be a man with an attitude, the angrier she got. "You probably think I'm stupid because I got caught in this miserable storm. I should have been paying attention to the weather, but I was too busy daydreaming about my future on the island. Normally, I'm very much in control of what I'm doing." Mikela put down her coffee mug with such force that coffee spilled onto the table. The dogs jumped up and came around to keep an eye on her.

"Easy Niska, Abby. Our guest is emotional from a hard day driving in a bad storm. A good night's sleep will calm her down." To Mikela he said, "I never raise my voice to the dogs. Your excitement startled them. They won't hurt you." He ruffled both dogs' necks and when they were satisfied that Mikela was not a danger to their master, returned to their floor cushion.

Mikela had taken a paper napkin from the center of the table and wiped up her spill. "I'm sorry," she sighed, crumpling up the napkin. "I guess I'm just worn out from this whole day. It's been a nightmare. I'm very grateful to you for taking me out of the storm and warming me up. I needed this break. I'd better get going before I wear out my welcome, if I haven't done that already." She pushed back her chair and got up, the dogs coming back to see what was happening. She ruffled both of their necks and picked up her purse. "Thanks again for your hospitality." She walked through the dark living room to her dripping coat and took it from the peg. She put it on and sighed, thinking to herself that braving the storm would be much better than making this guy angry. Who knew what he had planned on doing to her if she stayed? She cast a last look around, hoping for a final glimpse of the man whose eyes had held her interest such a short time earlier. He must have still been sitting at the kitchen table, relieved that this silly woman was out of his life! She turned back to the door to leave and walked straight into his chest. His immense form was leaning against the solid front door. He took her chin in his hand and lifted her face to his.

"Mikela Williams, you're not going anywhere!"

Chapter Two

Mikela's heart was pounding so fast she couldn't breathe. The touch of his rough hand on the smooth skin of her face was as exhilarating as it was frightening. He must have misjudged the distance between them in the darkness because when he spoke, his lips brushed hers, soft as a petal. He smelled of coffee and cedar. The reflection of the flames licking the logs in the fireplace was dancing in his eyes. She was mesmerized by the moment. The presence and scent of the man filled her senses as she stood for what seemed like an eternity. A cold, wet nose in the palm of her hand jolted her back to reality.

"Ah, I—ah…what do you mean?" Mikela stammered, putting her hands on her hips.

His hand slowly released its hold on her chin and he placed both hands on her shoulders. Laughing, he said, "I'm sorry, Mikela. I didn't mean to frighten you. Look. It's too dangerous outside for you to leave right now. If the causeway's open in the morning, then you can go. Maybe I can talk some sense into you then, okay?" He released his hold on her. "Come on, let me get my stuff out of the bedroom and you can sleep there. I'll use the couch. I'll even let you borrow one of the dogs for company. How's that sound?"

He put an arm on her shoulder and walked her to one of three open doors behind the fireplace. It was obviously a man's bedroom with a king-sized, wood frame bed taking up most of the space. There were a couple of dressers, a chair with a pair of jeans hanging over the back, and what appeared to be Ansel Adams photographs on the walls. On the nightstand were some small, framed photographs, a dish with a few coins in it and a paperback. He gave two short whistles and Abby came into the room and sat at the foot of the bed. Dropping her duffle bag onto the bed he said, "Sleep well, Mikela. I'll see you in the morning." From one of the dresser drawers he pulled out a pair of sweats. He looked back over his shoulder and smiled at her once again, and then stepping out of the doorway, he pulled the door closed behind him.

Mikela tip-toed to the door and listened for any sound that he was still outside. A moment later she could hear the sound of logs being added to the fire and knew he was as good as his word. She felt safe in this house, with this man, with his animals. She smiled to herself and unzipped the duffel bag, not quite sure of the meaning of the stirrings in her heart. She felt around for the giant t-shirt that doubled as her nightgown and pulled out the travel bag containing her toothbrush and toothpaste.

"What do you think, Miss Abby? Am I safe with you and your master?" She smiled down at the beautiful canine and stroked its fur. After kicking off her wet shoes and peeling off soaked socks, Mikela found the master bathroom. Her eyes were swollen and burning and she desperately needed some rest. She hoped she'd look better after getting some much-needed sleep. Too tired to shower, she quickly washed her face and brushed her hair. Her clothes littered the floor as she stripped and then pulled the huge tee shirt over her head. She picked the pile of clothes off the floor and set them on the chair, then got into bed and turned out the light. When her eyes adjusted to the dark, she saw Abby at the foot of the bed. Abby jumped up, turning in circles several times before settling down, her nose facing the doorway. Mikela pulled up the covers and snuggled in for the night, feeling the comforting pressure of Abby near her feet.

An irritating high-pitched noise was forcing Mikela out of her sound sleep. She tried rolling over and ignoring it, but it was just annoying enough to keep her awake. In a groggy stupor, she slowly realized that she didn't know where she was. This wasn't her apartment in New York, the sounds were different. She frantically tried to get her bearings. Nothing was familiar in the dim light. The nudge of a cold nose, followed by the licking of her cheek finally woke her out of her stupor. Mikela hugged Abby close to her body, still trying to place the awful sound. It would be terribly high-pitched and then suddenly lower in pitch only to rise again, like a quiet machinegun. Abby didn't seem concerned, so there couldn't be any real danger, could there? Mikela's curiosity got the better of her and she climbed as quietly as she could out of bed. She padded silently to the door and listened carefully for a few minutes. She could hear a man's voice, but couldn't be sure if it was Abby's master or not. She pulled the door open a few inches, hoping there wouldn't be any telltale creaking to give her away. She padded past a bathroom and leaned against the doorjamb of the next doorway. There he was, shirtless, wearing only the bottoms of a black sweatsuit. His back was to her as she watched him turning a knob that was causing the high and low pitched whining noise. He then plugged a set of headphones into the ham radio which sat nearby. The annoying noise was silenced. This room must be his office. He sat in front of a computer but his chair was turned a bit to reach the microphone of the ham radio. There were maps and charts on the walls and she noticed several tall file cabinets.

"I'm losing you, Steve. You're breaking up—shipment? What about the shipment? Repeat! How many guards? Roger that Steve. No problem—a few more weeks, buddy. Stay safe. We're too close to blow it now. –I'll smoke him myself—watch your back…right. 10-4…over and out, 73." He switched the radio off and removed the bulky earphones. Just then Abby barked and he jumped up, spinning around, and pointed a gun straight at Mikela's heart.

"Oh, no! Oh, my God!" Mikela's eyes grew as big as saucers as she backed away from the doorjamb. Her heart was in her throat, her breath coming in shallow, rapid bursts. She put her hands up to protect herself while slowly backing away from him. Not taking her eyes off him, she backed into the unyielding mass wall of the stone fireplace and couldn't move another inch. Mikela's final thought was that she didn't even know the name of the man who was going to kill her. Then she blacked out.

Chapter Three

"Mikela…Mikela, wake up, everything's all right…come on, girl, wake up!" Someone was holding her hand and slapping her wrist. Mikela moaned and rolled her head from side to side. Slowly opening her eyes, she looked into the dark eyes of the man who had been her rescuer and now may very well become her murderer. She bolted upright, and digging her heels into the mattress, pushed herself into a sitting position, remembering only the sight of a gun barrel pointed at her chest. Freeing her hand from his, she backed so close to the headboard that she was painfully aware of the intricately carved design of the wood on her back.

"What do you want from me?" she whispered. Abby jumped up on the bed and came over to Mikela. The woolly dog sat as Mikela wrapped her arms around it, feeling as if Abby were her only friend in the world.

"Mikela, you startled me, that's all. I was concentrating so hard that I didn't have time to think of who was behind me. Hey, I didn't shoot you, did I?" He flashed his dimples at her and made an attempt to hold her hand, but she pulled back, trying to make sense of what had happened.

"It's not funny. You could have killed me! I think I would have been a lot safer out in the storm than in here with you! I'd like to get dressed now and leave!" Mikela was fuming. She felt the heat rush to her face, embarrassed and angry with herself for trusting a stranger.

"Well, excuse me, lady!" The dimples disappeared. "Maybe you shouldn't go sneaking around someone's house in the middle of the night. Ever think of that?" His eyes narrowed and he spoke with restrained hostility. "Another idiotic woman out to prove she's as capable as a man, driving in the middle of the worst storm of the decade, wanting to turn a run-down, dangerous lighthouse into a home…I'm sure you don't want to get blind-sided by using some intelligence in planning your life!" He stood and ran a hand through his hair. Why was this silly woman affecting him like this?

"Well, I won't be bothering you any longer than it takes to get dressed and out of here. You can forget all about ever having met *this* idiotic woman!" Mikela huffed. Abby looked from her master to their upset guest. Mikela pushed past her host and stomped into the bathroom, slamming the door. A few seconds later, the door opened and she pushed past him again, sheepishly grabbed her duffel bag and went back inside. He stood there, his hands on his hips watching her try to maintain her dignity while stomping angrily past. His anger now subsiding, he realized there was something about this woman that made him want to protect her. And that was more danger than he needed! He couldn't afford to let anyone get close to his heart, not in his line of work. He needed to stay free of any emotional entanglements!

Mikela dropped her bag on the closed toilet seat. Glimpsing herself in the mirror, she started to cry. *That arrogant bastard. Who did he think he was?* A knock on the door startled her. "What?" she gulped. She sobbed at her reflection. She was a mess, her hair all wild, eyes red and puffy.

The door opened a couple of inches and a calm, deep voice said, "I'm going to make us a pot of coffee. Calm down, take a shower and then come out so we can talk. Okay?" Mikela sobbed, but didn't reply. "Please, Mikela."

"Okay."

The door closed. Mikela sniffed a few more times and then got control of herself. Tonight she'd be in her lighthouse. Her very own lighthouse! Partly disappointed at his remarks and the realization that she'd come close to losing her heart to a—a what? A drug dealer? A hit man? Another part of her was grateful that he'd soon be nothing but a bad memory. She needed to get away from this guy, obviously a chauvinist, who was trying to put her dreams to an end. Not just a dream-crushing male chauvinist, but some sort of underworld character as well. She didn't need anyone like that in her life. She wanted roots and romance and she was darn well going to have both! Bolstered from her mental recharge, she turned on the water and when it felt just right, she stepped into the shower.

The hot water felt good on her back. She stood a few minutes, letting it rain down on her head. She reached for her shampoo and soap— lathering herself all over while bathed in the comforting fragrances. She was starting to feel much better. She had a wonderful adventure and a great life ahead of her. She was more determined than ever to put this past twenty-four hours behind her. She would be very pleasant toward this man—*what was his name?*—and then say her goodbyes. And that would be that.

Grabbing a couple of towels, she wrapped one around her hair and twisted it on top of her head. With another she dried off and went about her usual routine. When she'd finally gotten a comb through her thick mane of hair and dressed, she decided to put on her makeup and treat this day as any other. She quickly removed all her personal items, re-packed them in her duffel bag and neatly hung both towels on the rack. She grabbed the previous day's clothes from the chair in the bedroom, stuffed those into her bag, tossed it by the door and then sat on the bed to pull on her socks. Mikela saw the door slowly opening and watched as Abby came to sit at her feet. Abby laid her head on Mikela's knees and looked up.

"Oh, Abby, I wish I could take you with me. I'm going to miss you, sweetheart." Mikela stroked the dog's head and bent over to whisper, "If I could think of a way to sneak you out of here, I would!" For a moment they touched noses and Mikela genuinely felt sad at the thought of leaving this gentle creature behind. She forced herself to stand and braced herself for the next encounter with the handsome, egotistical, headstrong and dangerous man of the house. She stepped into dried, but stiff, loafers and grabbed her duffel bag and purse. She headed for the kitchen and the smell of fresh brewed coffee.

He was pouring the coffee into mugs when she entered the kitchen.

She stood quietly and watched him, wondering what he could possibly want to talk about. Nothing he could say would sway her from her dream. Her heart skipped a beat when he turned to face her. He returned the pot to its hotplate and came toward her, arms outstretched. "Mikela, I'm sorry. I don't know why or how, but I care about you and don't want to see you get hurt. I really don't want you to leave." With that said, he took her in his arms and kissed her. Mikela's bags dropped to the floor with a thud. Adrenaline rushed through her body and she couldn't help her response. Her lips sought his with an urgency she hadn't felt in a long time and she wrapped her arms around his neck. Her heart was pounding in her chest, lips responding to this unexpected turn of events.

When he stopped for air, Mikela pushed him away. "You're unbelievable! One minute you try to kill me, the next minute you're kissing me. What's with you? You haven't even had the decency to tell me your name!" She went to the refrigerator and took out the milk. He said nothing, picking up the sugar and a spoon and set them in front of her on the table. He watched her in silence as she added milk and sugar and stirred furiously.

"Jim. Jim Strongheart."

Mikela looked up from her coffee and smiled. "Thank you, Jim Strongheart." Trying to sound casual, she added, "What did you want to talk about?" She kept stirring her coffee, trying to pretend a disinterest that she didn't feel. Physically, Jim Strongheart was her "dream man." He was tall, dark and muscular—someone you'd always feel safe with in a crowd. She could lose herself in his eyes—dark and mysterious, and once again, that animal magnetism was threatening to make her lose control of her emotions. She reminded herself of what she'd overheard when he was on the radio. The man was into something illegal and she had no intention of ruining her life with a loser, no matter how much she was attracted to him!

"Mikela, please don't keep looking away. I really wish you'd stay a while and think things through. You need to forget about that lighthouse, it's dangerous that far out on Beam Island. There have been murders and drug busts out there. It's way too isolated for a woman on her own. You don't need that kind of trouble. I'm going to be gone for a couple of days and you could stay here with Abby. I'll take Niska with me and you'd have time to figure out what to do. What do you think?" He earnestly sought her eyes, needing to connect with her. He couldn't explain the wrenching in his heart when he thought of the danger she might be putting herself into. There was something about this fearless woman with the wild hair that was making him think like a schoolboy with a crush on the prom queen.

"Jim, I really do appreciate your concern. I mean it. And I'd love to stay with Abby. But this is my parents' gift to me, my inheritance, and I'm going to make it my home. I've already decided my future. I don't exactly know everything that will happen in my life, but I've made my plans and I'm not one to change my mind. I'm grateful that you helped me out of the storm, but I really don't need any more help. I'll make it just fine. I want to finish what I've started out to do." Mikela took a sip of coffee and peeked over the rim of the cup at Jim. He was staring at her, a look of total disbelief on his face.

"You know, girl, you're nuts! I hope to hell you know what you're doing, because you're obviously too stubborn to take anyone's advice. Well, you go right ahead and get on with this future of yours and have a nice life. I've got to go. Take care of yourself."

He stood up from his chair, knocking it over in his frustration. He picked it up and slammed it back to its spot under the table. He stomped out the back door, never looking back, Niska at his heels.

Mikela sat, feigning calm, and finished her coffee. "Well, Abby, so much for your dad never raising his voice!" The sooner she was out of here and on the road, the happier she'd be. This guy had a volatile temper and she didn't want to get caught in it again. Grabbing her mug, she rinsed it out in the sink and set it in the drainer. She picked up her purse and found her notebook and pen and scribbled a quick note of thanks that she left on the counter. She stooped to pick up her bags and headed toward the front door and stopped to give sweet Abby another good stroking. Opening the front door, she stepped into the misty morning and was grateful that the wind and rain had moved on through the night. If she made good time and the weather behaved itself, she'd be at the lighthouse before noon!

As she put her duffel bag into the rear of the SUV, she kept hoping to catch one last glimpse of Jim Strongheart. He was nowhere in sight. She chided herself for the feeling of disappointment that tugged at her heart as she turned the last corner away from his home and headed back toward the highway.

Chapter Four

The heavy feeling in Mikela's heart lifted as she spotted the highway coming into view. The morning had broken gray and drizzly, but the storm had done its worst and now the clean up would begin. She passed rumbling yellow state highway department trucks alongside the highway, the workers wearing the same yellow raingear that Jim had worn when he'd saved her from the storm. She felt a wave of sadness remembering the way they'd parted. She'd really have to make herself forget about Jim Strongheart. She had a new life to begin. A new and exciting adventure lay before her and she wouldn't let anything hold her back. As she slowly passed by, she observed the workers, chainsaws and chippers whirring away, clearing the debris from the road. Frequently she had to slow down and even stop to wait for a large tree to be pulled from the center of the paved highway.

She had traveled in the stop-and-go traffic for almost an hour when at long last she passed over the bridge to Beam Island, making a grand entrance under the bridge's elaborate metal archway that proudly proclaimed *Welcome to Beam Island, Maine. Population: 66.* She smiled excitedly and felt like she'd entered a whole new world. The population would soon be sixty-seven she told herself. She tried to remember the lay of the little village. It wasn't too difficult, as nothing much had changed since the summer she had spent here with her parents. A new coat of paint here and there to cheer old wooden facades, but it was still the quaint little fishing village of her childhood. In summer months, tourists swelled the population to several thousand and supplied the incomes of the villagers. Most of the year-round villagers earned their living as bed and breakfast or hotel owners, crafts people, or by chartering fishing boats. There were several little restaurants featuring fabulous lobster and crab concoctions to be relished after an appetizer of world famous New England clam chowder. Brightly painted salt-water taffy stands dotted the road. She was searching Main Street looking for McHenry's, an old, family-owned store. She remembered a jam-packed wooden structure, loaded with every imaginable item, both edible and non. The towering shelves, stuffed from floor to ceiling, supplied the entire island with every possible necessity, its motto being, "If you don't see it, you don't need it." Mikela smiled as she spotted the sign over McHenry's Groc & Gas. Exactly as she remembered! She drove past the island's tiny post office and equally small library and pulled neatly into the lone parking space nestled between a highway patrol car and an old pick-up truck that had seen better days.

She went up the few wooden steps to the front porch of McHenry's. A weathered corkboard was still prominently fixed between the old-fashioned wooden and glass doors. A few scattered business cards along with a "Lost Kitten" sign and an upcoming bake sale to benefit the library were posted. She noticed that she'd missed the bake sale by a week. Mikela would make a list of all the items she'd need, but for now she would just pick up some supplies to hold her over for the next couple of days as she got herself situated in her new home. The smell of freshly brewed coffee was stirring up memories of Jim again and she followed her nose to a little beverage and snack area. Homemade breakfast treats and donuts were in a glass case and there were three little round tables with an assortment of chairs. One of the tables had two occupants; an older gentleman in well-worn denim overalls, the other a state trooper. Both men paused in their conversation to smile at her. "Well, hello there, little lady," said the older fellow with a twinkle in his eye. He twisted in his seat to get a good look at the newcomer. "I'll be danged, Ross, look what the storm blew in!"

Mikela laughed, "I could smell the coffee and pastries all the way from the mainland. I had to see where it would lead!" She walked to the coffee pot, pulled a Styrofoam cup from the tray and began pouring the steaming liquid.

"Sophie makes the best coffee on Beam!" the older fellow boasted. "That's why she can't get rid of us!"

"Who are you two harassing, now?" called a voice from behind a set of swinging doors. A broadly smiling gray-haired woman emerged from the doors, toting a tray of cinnamon rolls. "Well, who have we here?"

"Hi. Mikela Williams. I need some of your coffee and rolls before I starve to death." Mikela stirred milk and sugar into her coffee and took a roll from the glass case.

"Welcome, Mikela. I'm Sophie Norton and this old geezer is Otis, my husband." Sophie laughed as she good-naturedly elbowed her husband. "This good lookin' fella is Ross Daniels, our resident state trooper. Now you boys make Mikela welcome." Otis and Ross nodded and murmured 'hello's'. Sophie's apple red cheeks reminded Mikela of good health and sunshine. "Now why don't you tell us what brings you to Beam?" Sophie's sea-blue eyes were clear and direct. She was a stout, buxom little woman with a ready smile and an engaging manner. Mikela was charmed by the warmth and friendliness of this couple and set her coffee and roll down on the next table. Ross stood up as Mikela neared and smiled once again, showing even, white teeth. His interest in the newcomer was not escaping Mikela, although she couldn't quite determine if it was his line of work that made him interested or perhaps he found her attractive.

"Well, I'm not sure where to begin. My parents left me a place here on the island and I'm moving in. That's pretty much the whole story in a nutshell. Unfortunately, I drove right into the storm yesterday and got waylaid overnight. But I made it!" She took several long swallows of the rich, brown liquid and could feel the warmth spreading throughout her body.

"Yer lucky ya didn't get washed away. That was one of the worst I ever seen in these parts—and I been here a mighty long time, "said Otis, Sophie nodding her head in agreement. Mikela took a bite of the fresh baked cinnamon roll. It was still warm from the oven and the most delicious thing she could ever remember tasting. She washed it down with another long sip of coffee.

"Yes, thank goodness, I had some help on the highway. I've only been back on the road for an hour or so. The state crews seem to have everything under control," she smiled at Sophie.

"Who are your parents? Don't tell me the Langleys, now, girl, 'cause those city slickers didn't have the moxie to stick it out here for very long!" Otis snorted. Ross helped himself to another cup of coffee and sat back down.

Sophie sat next to Mikela and patted the younger woman's arm. Mikela smiled. "No, it was the Williams. John and Christa Williams. They owned the lighthouse. Bought it back in the 70s. In fact we all came out together and spent a summer here, but that was years ago. I don't know if you'd remember them or not. They never got to use it very much."

Mikela noticed that a momentary shadow crossed Ross' face. "Did you say the lighthouse?" He looked around at Sophie and Otis, then back at Mikela. "I don't want to discourage you, but that might be a lot more trouble than you bargained for."

Mikela watched Ross over the top of her coffee cup. Tall and lean with a light complexion, he was the opposite of Jim in looks. His eyes looked like grey steel and made an odd contrast to his short-cropped, sand-colored hair. His face was all hard angles, not a look of softness anywhere. Still, when he smiled there was something attractive about him.

"That seems to be the popular opinion," Mikela sighed, remembering Jim's warning. "I've saved enough money to fix it up and I intend to make it my home. I think it'll be wonderful living in a lighthouse with only the sound of the waves for company at night. It will be a good project for me anyway. I already bought several how-to books. I wanted to do most of the remodeling myself. Hopefully, it won't be too difficult to get the place in shape and once that's done, I can figure out what to do with the rest of my life." She smiled around at all of them, hoping she sounded as fearless as she intended.

Sophie got up and reached for the never-empty coffee pot. She refilled cups all around and got another pot ready to brew. Thoughtfully she asked, "You mean you're here all by yourself? You're not married? Honey, just what are you going to do with yourself once you've got the lighthouse all cozy? If you're looking for a man out here, there's mighty slim pickin's, as they say. Present company excluded, of course!" She gave Ross a wink and a grin. "Most folks out here run family businesses, Mikela. Have you thought it out? 'Course it's none of my business, but maybe you're rich. Did I mention that Ross is single?" Sophie's grin lit up the room and warmed Mikela's heart.

A quick look in Ross' direction showed his mock exasperation. "Don't worry, Ross. I'm very happy as a single girl. But it looks like Sophie's one relentless matchmaker. Why is it that every married woman I know just won't believe that single people can be happy too?" Mikela tried to make light of the subject and hoped Sophie wouldn't belabor the point. She didn't know anyone in the room well enough to joke about her non-existent social life. And she hadn't quite shaken her attraction for Jim yet, either. Of course, a nice diversion might do the trick as far as making her forget about Jim Strongheart.

Mikela wadded up her napkin and put it inside her Styrofoam coffee cup, taking her trash to the nearby container. "I thank you all for the good company, but I'm eager to get on my way and see the lighthouse while I've got most of the daylight to work with. Sophie, I need a few groceries and supplies to last for a couple of days and then I'll be back with a big list. It was really great meeting you, Otis and Ross." Mikela handed Sophie a list from her purse as Otis gave both ladies a wink and wriggled his eyebrows at Ross. Ross rolled his eyes and stood up, walking after Mikela and Sophie. Sophie and the list stopped every few feet, grabbed something from the shelves and continued heading toward the front doors as Ross caught Mikela's elbow and stopped her.

"Mikela, I'll escort you out to the lighthouse and make sure you get safely inside. I doubt anyone's been out there in several years. You might run into vandals or rodents and need a hand." Ross had taken her arm when making his statement. He was a little too close for Mikela's comfort, but she brushed the thought away. He was just being helpful and neighborly.

Mikela made a step backward and smiled up at Ross. "Thank you, Ross, but it's not necessary. I hope I'm not being silly, but this is sort of a personal quest I've been on and I really need to be alone the first time I walk in there. I hope you understand. I've got a lot of memories of my parents to deal with and I want to be alone with them for a few days."

A moment of silence lingered between them. Ross didn't seem pleased but put on his hat, touched the brim and said, "No problem, Mikela. I'm sure Otis will let me know in a day or two if you made it." His remark almost sounded like a warning, but again, Mikela brushed it off. *Just another macho guy trying to protect a little lady*, she thought to herself.

"I think I've got everything here, Mikela," Sophie called from behind several bags of groceries. She waved after Ross as he walked through the front doors and whispered to Mikela, "Well, any dinner plans? Now don't mind me, honey, I've got to give everybody a hard time. It's just in my blood!" Sophie giggled as Mikela shook her head and laughed.

"I think you and I are going to get along just fine, Sophie." Mikela grinned. In a conspiratorial whisper, she said, "Ross offered to come up with me, but I told him I needed to be alone with my memories for a couple of days. I also need to get the place presentable in case I have a visitor! Thank you for getting all this together for me, Sophie. You're a doll." Mikela took out her wallet and put several twenty dollar bills on the counter. Waving away the compliments, Sophie rang up the sale on the old-fashioned cash register and handed Mikela her change. "I'll see you in a couple of days. I'll need more of those cinnamon rolls by then!" she laughed. Otis came from the back of the store and scooped up the grocery bags, walking Mikela out to her SUV. As they loaded her supplies into the rear of the vehicle and made small talk, Mikela spied a highway patrol car parked in an alley across the street, seemingly hidden from view. Otis opened the door for her and made her promise to give a full report in a couple of days, or he'd send a posse out to find her.

Mikela laughed with Otis, and waved goodbye to Sophie who'd come out on the front porch. "I'll see you soon," she called out, and backing out of her parking space, put her vehicle into gear, starting the final leg of her journey. She pointed her vehicle toward the far end of the island, noticing what appeared to be gathering storm clouds in the distance. She grimaced as she said a silent prayer for a quick trip with no surprises awaiting her at the lighthouse. As she took a last look in the rearview mirror, she saw Ross Daniels scowling, hands on his hips at the side of his patrol car, watching her drive into the storm.

Chapter Five

Mikela followed Main Street as it led away from town, threading its way through the little community. Near the edge of town the pavement changed from asphalt to gravel as the road became narrower, little more than a well-traveled path that wound a maze through picturesque summer cottages. As it meandered up a small incline, she took note of the various shops and businesses, most of them closed this time of year. Many of the homes had business signs in their front yards as well. *Nan's House of Beauty* was also *Seaton's Tax Service.* The villagers probably all wore several hats in their attempts at making a living in a tourist area with only the brief summer season bringing in real revenues. As she crested the hill, the road opened onto a majestic view of the island's oldest and most famous structure, the Glenhaven Hotel. Even with the gathering dark storm clouds it was impressive. It had been a sprawling, regal sight in the 1920s and 30s, boasting many famous visitors and summer guests. It looked like a massive White House, all columns and white moldings three stories high. It was situated on one of the highest areas above sea level on the island, second only to the lighthouse itself. She idled at the stop sign, taking in the view. A right turn would take her on a trek of two miles to the island's resort marinas, while a left would take her along the edge of the bluffs, past a small white-washed, wood-framed church, still in use after 200 years. Several summer cottages were scattered among the bluffs and each million-dollar home boasted glorious views. Much of the island had been designated as a natural wildlife refuge and there were many hiking trails and picnic areas and little fresh-water ponds surrounded by reeds, native grasses and shrubs. Birds and rabbits shared the breathtaking views with the tourists. Mikela turned toward the bluff side of the road, while making a mental note to hike down to the beach at the foot of the bluffs at her first opportunity.

She drove on around the last corner of the wildlife area and suddenly there it was, jutting through a canopy of parted trees. Even in the gloom the lighthouse loomed up out of the mist like a surly stone sentinel, the black clouds gathering around its uppermost level, the mist swirling around its body. Its footing was the edge of a bluff and huge sea-tumbled stones anchored its base. For a moment, Mikela fought the urge to turn around and drive back to the safety of Otis and Sophie's store. She chided herself for being silly. It was so much more imposing than she remembered, not the romantic vision she'd kept in her heart all these years.

The drive in front of her stretched along for almost half a mile. Rutted in places, soft sand in others, she bobbed and weaved the SUV around the largest of the potholes, careful not to leave the pathway in case the sand would swallow her up. She tried to fight back her rising fear. The lighthouse was so much more formidable than she remembered, making her feel small and afraid. She'd been dreaming of walking into a warm and welcoming conversation piece, a place that she would lovingly re-decorate and call home, comforting and secure. Nothing about this monstrous rock structure struck her as comforting or secure! She told herself it was just the gathering storm that made it appear so menacing as the bolts of lightning backlit the scene like a very real nightmare. Mikela pulled the SUV up to the single, rounded door at the island side of the bluff and turned off the engine. She stared for a moment, wondering if the shadows at the very top were ghosts of former occupants or just an overactive imagination. She let out a deep sigh as she reached into her glove compartment for the ancient brass key that would unlock the heavy wooden door.

"Here goes nothing," Mikela whispered to herself as she slowly exited the vehicle. The wind whipped up, slamming her door shut. Mikela's nerves rattled as she grabbed her purse tighter to her body. She made a dash to the front door, hovering under the tiny eave for protection as she fumbled with the old skeleton key in the lock. She could hear the lock groan and creak under the pressure from the key and knew she'd unlocked it, but the door refused to budge. She pushed on it several times without making any progress and finally flung her full weight onto the moisture-swollen wood. The door flew open and Mikela felt herself propelled along by her weight down a small stairway, painfully connecting her shoulder with each of the six steps. Afraid to move until she was sure she hadn't broken any bones, she listened to her breathing echo off the stone walls of the lighthouse chamber. A lightning bolt made shadows come alive as she tried to calm her beating heart and gather her thoughts. In the darkness, she determined that nothing felt numb or particularly painful to her touch, so she doubted that anything was broken. She rubbed her left shoulder which had taken the brunt of her tumble and decided she was only bruised and would be sore for couple of days. A long, low rumble belched from the storm and Mikela noted that the lighthouse was just as solid as the bedrock it was built on. She certainly wouldn't fear any bad weather in here! Overhead she heard the rain pelting the metal and glass where the old beacon had been housed. In her fantasies of the lighthouse, she had imagined a room at the very top, library shelves wound around the outside perimeter. Lots of light meant lots of hanging plant baskets. A wonderful refuge where she'd read and write to her heart's content. In the lightning's brief illumination, she saw only the crusty designs embedded over the years by salt spray on the glass and what appeared to be lots of rust.

Mikela slowly raised herself to a sitting position. She groped around in the dim light for her handbag and once she found it, she held on to it like a life preserver. Rising to her full height and standing firmly on her feet, she rubbed her shoulder once again, wincing with the pain. She'd smacked herself pretty hard on the steps and vowed to slow down from here on out. Deciding to unload her supplies and camping gear first, she climbed the stairs to the door and got behind the wheel of the SUV. She backed its rear end up to the doorway, so she'd be able to unload her supplies without getting soaked to the skin. She'd leave the truck parked where it was overnight so she wouldn't have to worry about locking the door again and getting trapped inside.

After several trips to the car, Mikela had the contents of the vehicle unloaded in the center of the first floor. She unpacked her big six-volt lantern and set it up as her main source of light as she found and unpacked her various camping lamps. She felt a little more confident once the room was free of shadows. She didn't fear the storm in the solid building and now she didn't fear the shadows the lightning had made dance around the room, either. She up-ended the milk crates she'd packed her things in and used them as a makeshift table and chair. For today, she'd just work on the main floor and see exactly what furnishings she had to work with.

Slowly she turned in a circle in the center of the room and shone the flashlight in front of her. She started with the entry door and wooden stairway she'd tumbled down and moved to the left. The lighthouse had a dozen small windows, set into the stone about ten feet above the floor. Even in broad daylight, Mikela doubted they'd shed much light into this central room. Toward the ocean side of the building, there were several closed doors that needed exploring. She kept turning and smiled as her light stopped on the old fireplace, remembering how proud her parents had been of the Yankee craftsmanship of the curved oak mantle. At the far edge of the fireplace was a little closet, set underneath the steps that led to the door. The tiny closet had been used as storage for their beach chairs.

Mikela set off in search of the kitchen and tried the center door first. It opened easily, creaking on its long-unused hinges. She welcomed the window over the kitchen sink and stood for a moment, lost in memories of her mom and dad and all the yard sales they'd stopped at to find the furniture they'd bought to make this old lighthouse their little summer get-away. The fifties-styled Formica table with chrome legs was still there, surrounded by three almost-matching chairs. Duct tape had been used to repair a couple of tears in the vinyl coverings.

Her parents had had the kitchen fitted with a small, but modern, cookstove and tiny electric refrigerator. The door to the fridge was still propped open and Mikela smiled as she recognized her mom's handiwork—a lone box of baking soda sitting on the top shelf so there wouldn't be any odors

when it was next used. There were two separate areas of cabinets; each
with two rows of shelves and glass doors, still holding the family's melamine
camping dinnerware, a red and white gingham pattern. Mikela opened
one of the doors and took down a coffee cup, again a child, relishing the
memory of the 'special' coffee her mom would make just for her. Half
coffee, half milk, two teaspoons of sugar. She'd made it weak for a
child's stomach, but it was real coffee, making Mikela feel like a grown-
up. To this day, Mikela took her coffee "light and sweet." A loud crack
followed by a dazzling flash of light that electrified the room made her
jump. The little cup hit the floor and rolled around in circles, slowly coming to a stop. Jolted out of her reverie, Mikela picked it up and placed it
back on the shelf.

Mikela spent the rest of the afternoon unpacking the items she'd brought
along and made a makeshift bed in the main room. She'd brought an
inflatable mattress and air pump that took a considerable amount of time
to inflate. When that was done, she laid her sleeping bag over it and
would use her duffel bag for a pillow. Sitting on one of the crates, she
took out her journal and made notes from her experiences of the last two
days. She started her shopping list and on another page drew a circle, a
makeshift plan of the lighthouse, filling in the areas of her new home as
best she could. She would explore the rest of the lighthouse tomorrow
morning and see what the upper levels held in store for her. But she would
wait for the sunlight to come with her. It was getting chilly in the stone
structure and Mikela's stomach was complaining from lack of food. She
wished she had another cup of coffee to warm her up, but until she had
her utilities turned on and the chimney flue checked, she didn't want to
start any kind of fire. She dug around in one of the grocery bags from
McHenry's and located bottled water and another one of Sophie's cinnamon rolls. Her hand found an unfamiliar package and she lifted it out.
Written on the Styrofoam lid of the carton was *Welcome Mikela!* Mikela
opened the lid and inhaled deeply. Homemade lasagna with two slices of
buttered bread! Mikela was touched by Sophie's thoughtful gesture and
equally glad she was alone and unwatched as she ravenously attacked her
new friend's gift.

When she'd had her fill, she took the flashlight and decided to look behind the two remaining closed doors on either side of the kitchen. The first opened into a small, compact bathroom. It consisted of a shower stall, commode and sink. There were wooden shelves above the commode and a cabinet up against the inside wall. She found linens, extra shampoo and toiletries inside. The mirrored medicine cabinet over the sink was old and moisture had taken its toll on the backing. When she pulled on its door, a dead spider fell into the sink. Thinking twice about doing anything more without the electricity turned on, she moved her flashlight all around the bathroom and seeing that the commode had been winterized, she'd need to hire a handyman as soon as possible to make sure all the pipes and fixtures were still in good shape. Delicate webs crisscrossed the small enclosure and she decided her next visit to the bathroom would be armed with a vacuum cleaner.

She closed the door on the bathroom and went to the remaining door of what had been her parents' room. She slowly pushed it open and shone her light inside. The beam illuminated a bedstead and bureaus. The quilt her grandmother had made still lay draped over the foot of the bed. She saw the walk-in closet door, but decided to wait until she had better light. No telling what had found its way inside over the last decade. Spiders were not her favorite critters and she certainly didn't want to deal with them in the dark.

Returning her attention to the main room, she slid two heavy items of camping gear near the little closet under the steps, where they would be out of the way. She'd brought her camp sink and chemical commode. It would be fun to "rough it" for a day or two. She'd make the best of the situation and pretend she was on a camping trip. She had to kneel to wash in the tiny portable sink, but she managed to get ready for bed.

She slid into her sleeping bag and punched the duffel bag "pillow" a few times, trying to make it comfortable. As Mikela switched off the last of her lanterns, she felt something stir in the still air above her head. Her terror-filled eyes saw nothing in the pitch blackness that enveloped her, but she could sense a presence coming toward her. Directly behind her now, like the sound of a thousand demons from hell came the low, insistent moan "whoooooooo, whooooooooooo…" It was an awfully long time before she finally fell asleep.

Chapter Six

Three a.m. Mikela slept fitfully, waking up disoriented throughout the night. The waves breaking over the rocks, along with the rhythm of the ocean, the ebb and flow of the tide would lull her to sleep. But sleep would not last, and she'd find herself awakened by uneasy thoughts and strange noises. She finally gave up trying to force herself to sleep.

She wriggled deeper into the warmth of the sleeping bag, letting her thoughts wander back to the day she received the news that her parents had been involved in a serious accident. She'd been in Paris at the time, waiting on an urgent package to be delivered back to the United States. She took the first flight back, asked the taxi driver to wait while she signed off on the package at WorldTron, Inc. and went straight to the hospital. The emergency room doctor met her and broke the tragic news. She had been too late. Mikela was dumb-struck. She walked through the next two weeks in a smothering fog, moving like a zombie during the funeral services, paperwork and legalities. He parents had left her well-provided for through their life insurance policies. Not rich, but comfortable enough to buy a new vehicle and take a year's leave of absence from her job. She sold the contents of her parent's apartment, keeping a few family keepsakes that she treasured and decided to fulfill her parents' dream of making the lighthouse into a home.

The image of Jim Strongheart meandered into Mikela's thoughts. How safe she felt with him, the comfort of his home and how his wonderful bundle of wool, Abby, had stolen her heart. She couldn't help but smile to herself remembering the sweet dog that had befriended her. One thought led to another and she found herself remembering Jim's kiss, the warmth of his embrace. She felt herself wishing for the comfort of his arms around her now.

Oh, but she couldn't feel this way. She'd overheard his conversation and knew he was involved in something illegal. Something that sounded a lot like murder. And then there were his warnings about the lighthouse. He may have been attracted to her, but he wasn't really interested. He thought she was just a silly woman, trying to prove herself. He didn't know a thing about her or her life. She'd been proud of herself when she realized she hadn't thought about him at all her first day at the lighthouse. Now, however, she was letting him into her nighttime thoughts.

She tried to switch gears in her mind, thinking back to her visit at McHenry's store. The friendliness of Sophie and Otis, the way Ross Daniels had looked at her and offered to take her home.

Breaking the stillness of the night, she heard what she supposed was the same owl that had scared her earlier, not hooting now, but flying almost silently far above her head. She could sense his presence in the lighthouse. Not one to believe in ghosts, she made a mental note to see what was living in the higher levels soon. She imagined there were many birds and possibly other critters that had made the deserted lighthouse their home in the last decade.

The sound of the waves breaking over the rocks was joined by a high-pitched wail. Mikela sat up in her sleeping bag and listened closely. She couldn't be sure but it sounded like a woman crying, her voice carrying on the wind that had started up again during the early morning hours. Mikela's heart beat faster. She dressed quickly in the clothes she'd taken off just a few hours earlier and slipped into her loafers. Grabbing her flashlight, she went slowly up the steps to the front door. She put her ear to the door and listened quietly. The wail would stop and then start up again.

She pried the front door open and slipped between the lighthouse and the back of her SUV. It was still black in the early morning hours, the moon playing hide and seek with the clouds rolling rapidly overhead. She tried to stay in the shadows, adjusting her eyes to the dark night. She didn't see anyone as she scanned the area around her so she slipped the flashlight into her pocket. The origin of the sound was hard to pinpoint, but she followed it as best she could. As she approached the bluff side of the grounds, she searched for a trail of some sort that would lead her down to the beach below. The tide must have been going out, since the beach was visible to her from her 75 foot vantage point. She recalled when it was high tide, there was only ocean all around on three sides of the lighthouse.

She groped through the sparse cover of trees, slipping from one scrub cedar to the next as she looked for a trail or deer path, following the sound as best she could. At last she saw a clearing with a bit of railing leading down the side of the bluff. Making sure there was no human being in her range of vision, she started down the sand path that wove among the outcropping of rocks and grasses, steep in some places, leveling out in others. The wooden railing was rickety at best and Mikela tried to hug the rocks in the tight spots, using fingers and feet, rather than lean her weight onto the railing.

She heard a deep whooshing, sucking sound, increasing in volume the closer she got to the beach. It seemed to be coming from the same place as the wailing. Someone was trapped on the beach! As she worked her way around an outcrop of the bluff, her fingers found a crack in the rock to hold but her left foot couldn't make contact with anything solid. She tried leaning as far out to her left as she could stretch and finally her left shoe felt something hard. Mikela realized that she must have found a cave of some sort. She very carefully managed to get the flashlight out of her pocket and into her left hand. She turned the light on and scanned the area to her left.

She must have discovered the caves that Jim had told her about. Only about six feet above ground, the entry would be under water when the tide rolled in. She shone the light directly below her and realized she could make it to the ground climbing down the rocks directly below where she was perched. She clicked off the flashlight and put it back in her jacket pocket. Slowly, still feeling with her feet and fingers, she managed to climb backwards down the rest of the bluff's rocky face.

When she felt sand below her feet, she breathed a sigh of relief. Mikela was not particularly fond of heights! She walked to the black gaping mouth of the cave entrance and saw that it could be entered much more easily from the other side, where the rocks made a natural ladder and could be easily climbed. The wailing started up again as she began her climb into the entryway. It was wet and slippery where she walked but Mikela didn't dare to call out to the woman yet. She walked slowly and carefully further into the darkness, keeping one hand on the rock wall. The whooshing noise was almost deafening as it echoed throughout the cavern walls.

Mikela lost the last bit of illumination from the moon and decided to risk the flashlight. She turned it on and could see that the path she was on opened into a much larger room. As she stepped into the large chamber, she found the cause of the whooshing noise. There was a tidal pool inside the large cavern and as the tide ebbed and flowed, it made a whirlpool toward the center that must empty into another part of the cave or even into the ocean itself. She shone the flashlight around the huge, cavern room. Damp and cool, she could feel a breeze coming from another part of the cavern. She followed what looked like a natural stone path that led to the far end of the chamber.

The wailing voice was coming from what she guessed would be directly under the lighthouse. She slowly walked behind the flashlight's beam, careful of her footing, following the trail for another ten minutes before it split. The left path emptied into another large room, while the right appeared to get smaller and narrower. Mikela noticed that the wailing had stopped. She now wondered whether what she heard was a woman or maybe just the wind as it whipped along the walls of this mysterious cave. Jim had told her that people had long told of hearing the ghosts of Native American women at the lighthouse. Mikela wondered if it was just the wind that added to the tall tale told to warn her off the island. The sucking noise had almost stopped as well. Perhaps when the tidal pool emptied, the noises ceased altogether.

She didn't want to pursue her search any farther without telling someone where she was. If she slipped and broke a leg, the tide would come up and drown her long before anyone would think of looking for her.

Mikela decided to head back to the lighthouse. She would talk to Sophie in the morning and tell her about the wailing. Maybe Ross would be at the store and she could find out what he knew about the caves, too. As she turned she saw a glimmer of light bobbing up and down and then the sound of male voices reached her ears. Someone else was in the cave! Mikela could hear her heart pounding and feared that whoever was coming toward her would hear it, too. She groped in the dark and prayed that the narrow path would not be the one taken by whoever was coming. Footsteps were getting louder and louder, echoing on the walls all around her. She knew the men were at the closest end of the cavern coming down the path. She ducked into the narrow passageway, stepping back several feet and prayed they'd walk on by.

The footsteps stopped just in front of her. "Can't you make it a half hour without lighting up? What the hell's a'matter with you anyway?" growled a low, craggy voice.

"Shut up, will ya? If we're surprising them idiots tonight, you'd better hope we beat 'em in here, cos your damn voice'll warn 'em!" A fit of coughing erupted.

"Then get moving. Like any moron can't smell that cigarette."

"You jes' shut up and be ready for a fight. I'm half-expectin' a double cross. Don't trust that Injun fella. Somethin's wrong about him. He's got them squirrelly eyes." The footsteps started up again, their squabble temporarily forgotten, the footsteps heading farther and farther away from Mikela's hiding spot.

Mikela's heart was still pounding in her chest but she breathed a slow sigh of relief as the sound of their footsteps died out. She had to decide whether to keep hidden or try and get out of the cave as fast as her feet would carry her. Would the people they were meeting come from the same entrance? Maybe they were already inside. Or was there another way into the caverns? Mikela silently prayed for help with a quick decision. She wished she'd listened to Jim. Why did she have to be so stubborn about things?

She decided to make a run for it and get back to the safety of the lighthouse. It was pitch black inside the passageway and she'd either have to feel her way back to the big chamber or risk using the flashlight. She decided to feel her way into the big room. Once there, she'd have enough moonlight to find her way out and then back up the bluff. She hadn't noticed any footprints on the path when she'd climbed down the bluffs, so the men probably came in from the other side, or possibly in a boat.

Mikela made it through the large chamber without running into anyone. She scrambled out to the mouth of the cave and dropped down the six feet into the soft sand. The wind knocked out of her, she had to lie still for a few moments until she could catch her breath. As she lay with her head resting on the cool, wet sand, a flash of light shone straight into her eyes, totally blinding her. "Oh, no…" she managed, between gasps for air, her lungs still feeling as if they would burst.

"Well, well, well… if it isn't Mikela Williams. Just what the hell are you doing here?"

Chapter Seven

The bright light was extinguished and Mikela took her hands from her eyes, and laid them across her stomach. She took several deep breaths before trying to speak. "Oh, Jim," she whispered. "Thank God it's you. I was so afraid you were the guys meeting those creeps in the cave."

Jim stooped to pick Mikela up, one arm under her head, the other under her knees, cradling her in his arms. "I *am* one of the guys those creeps are meeting." Mikela hugged his neck, her face buried in his collar. He waited until she turned to look at him and pressed his lips to hers in a lingering kiss. He walked with her in his arms away from where she'd fallen and Mikela realized there were several men gathered at the cave's entrance. "I miss you, Mikela." Mikela caressed his face, feeling the day's growth of beard that had rubbed her cheek. She took his chin in her hand and turned his face back toward hers, exploring his mouth with her own.

Like an afterthought, the meaning of Jim's words came to Mikela. She pushed away from his chest and he set her upright, but did not relinquish his hold on her. "What do you mean you *are* the guys meeting those creeps?" she demanded.

"You and I need to talk, Mikela. I want to tell you about my job and the conversation you overheard. But I can't do it now. I need you to go back to the lighthouse and lock yourself in. I don't know how long it will be before I can get back here. It might be a few hours or a few days." Jim cupped her face in his hands, kissing her eyes, her cheeks, her lips, in-between his words. "You have to trust me." They were wrapped in each other's arms, savoring the moment. "I have to go now." They walked silently, arm in arm to the bluff face. Jim picked Mikela up by her waist and helped her to get her footing onto the narrow path she'd climbed down. "I'll be back, Mikela." He turned and walked away, joining the shadows at the mouth of the cave's entrance.

Mikela stood precariously balanced on the little path, watching until the last of the shadows disappeared into the cave. She felt an ache in her heart, wishing Jim hadn't gone. She had so many questions about this man. If she didn't still have sand in her mouth from the fall she'd taken, she would have thought this morning's adventures were all a crazy dream. She picked her way up the incline of the pathway, making very slow progress. She noticed that going down was much easier than climbing back up. The image of Jim kept creeping back into her thoughts as she found her way along the moonlit path through the trees and back to the lighthouse. What could he possibly explain to her about being a—a drug runner? She still couldn't imagine what type of underworld figure he was. What she overheard at his house sounded like he was going to kill some- one. Could he be an assassin? Whatever it was and whatever attraction she felt for him, she didn't want to end up with a man who was going to spend most of his adult life in a prison cell. Or worse yet—dead. Her thoughts strayed to the two dogs at his house. What had he done with them? Were they alone at his house, possibly for a week? How could she love a man that left his animals alone like that? The answer was simple—she couldn't, no matter how sexually attractive she found him!

Mikela squeezed around the rear of the SUV and into the lighthouse. She locked the door, hoping it would be easier to unlock than the first time. It would be daylight soon and she needed to clean up and head into town, find out what she could about the lighthouse's history and make arrangements to have her utilities turned on. Mostly she needed to talk to Sophie and feel like she had a connection on the island. Some good coffee and hot food in her stomach would help clear up the fog in her head.

She lit her camping lanterns as she had earlier in the night and took out her notebook. She made a list of the arrangements that would need to be made today. Telephone, electricity, trash removal, satellite dish, plumber. Once she had the utilities on, she would make a list of furnishings that would be needed. While trying to keep her thoughts in check, her heart wouldn't let her forget about Jim. She wanted to make this home a haven and wanted Jim to feel its warmth when he came to see her. She needed to show him that she wasn't the idiot that he thought she was. She wanted him to know that she could change this deserted, old lighthouse into a cozy home. She conjured up the image of the two of them sitting in front of the fire, the dogs lying on the hearth rug. Mikela started to smile, but then thought better of the turn her mind was taking and decided to get ready for town. It would take a while to get washed up in her little camping sink.

Mikela checked her watch and saw that it was 6:15. Putting her notebook into her purse, she realized she hadn't bothered to find out what time McHenry's opened, but hoped it was early. She desperately needed the comfort of breakfast and hot coffee. She took the steps up to the door and murmured another silent prayer that the door would open easily. Turning the key in the lock, she heard a click, and pulled on the heavy door. Nothing happened. She pulled again with all her might and it gradually let go of the door frame. She made another mental note to call a carpenter to have the door planed down to work more smoothly in the frame. The years of sea spray, rain and storms must have swollen the wood. She squeezed between the door and the SUV. She decided not to try and lock the door, but rather pushed it close. If no one had broken in for over a decade, it was doubtful that anyone would try today.

Mikela climbed into the SUV and sat for a few moments, savoring the beauty of the sun rising over the water's edge. Seagulls swirled lazily in the morning air, making their raucous calls. She shifted the vehicle into *drive* and headed back to town, visions of Jim, the caves and her new home flitting through her head.

Chapter Eight

Morning seemed to be a long time in coming as Mikela made her way through the wildlife refuge area and wound around the sleepy little cottages and homes on the island. The sky was still overcast from the passing storm and she couldn't decide if it looked like more rain or just more gloom. Her headlights would startle the birds as she came around corners, seagulls mostly, running from the waves on the beach, picking at the abundant breakfast tossed ashore by last night's angry ocean. Unlucky horseshoe crabs, fish and seaweed littered what she could see of the beach as she passed.

Mikela sighed deeply. Her heart was weary from the conflicting emotions she was feeling toward Jim Strongheart and the frightening events of the last few days. Add to her emotions the resulting lack of sleep and she was running on raw nerves. Nearing the little town, her spirits lifted as she thought of the hot coffee and good company to be found at McHenry's Groc & Gas. Mikela pulled into the same parking space she'd had on her first visit and smiled at a fisherman climbing into a battered pickup truck. After he drove away, she opened her door and grabbed her purse. She scooted out of the driver's seat and heard someone shout "Hey, lady!" Mikela turned to find the owner of the voice, Ross Daniels, waving at her. Mikela smiled and waved back. Ross crossed the street in a few quick steps and caught up to her. He took off his trooper's hat, holding it under his arm.

"How are you, Ross?" Mikela asked. She noticed that once again, he'd taken her elbow as they walked together. She admired his starched uniform and polished boots. Not one hair touched his collar. Ramrod straight posture. She imagined that he had a 'place for everything and everything in its place', just as her CPA father had. He took off his mirrored aviator sunglasses and slid one long ear piece into his shirt pocket, neatly folding the eyepieces to rest on the outside of his shirt. It didn't escape Mikela's notice that he was one good-looking state trooper!

"Just fine, Mikela. How'd you make it through yesterday's storm?" Ross took the wooden steps just ahead of her and held the door open as she walked through. He gave her an intense looking-over as she passed in front of him. "You look a little tired," he noted.

"Yes, well, I am tired. I was scared to death a couple of times last night so I didn't get much sleep. It's amazing how ghostly an old owl can sound when you're lying in a strange place in total darkness," laughed Mikela. Together they walked to the tables at the rear of the store. Ross held out her chair as Mikela sat down.

"Let me tell Sophie and Otis we're out here. I know they're concerned about you and will want to get all the details of your first night as an islander." Ross squeezed Mikela's shoulder and disappeared into the back room. The touch of his hand made her feel better. She wanted to respond to Ross, but she couldn't get Jim out of her mind. *Wait for me, Mikela,* he'd said. She could hear familiar voices, but couldn't quite make out the words. She held her head in her hands for a few moments, closed her eyes and hoped that the burning sensation would ease up. She thought she must look awful, but couldn't muster up the energy to do much about her appearance.

"Oh, honey, you must be exhausted!" Sophie leaned over Mikela, giving her a big hug. "Ross said you didn't get any sleep. What happened? Are you alright?"

Otis came over to the table with a tray holding four cups of coffee and set one down for each of them. Ross sat back in his own chair and pushed the sugar and milk pitcher in front of Mikela while Sophie hovered over them all like a mother hen. Danish and rolls were placed in the center of the table and finally, Otis and Sophie sat down. No one said a word. All eyes were expectantly on Mikela who was unaware of their scrutiny as she doctored her coffee. She took a long sip and looked up. Three sets of serious eyes were staring at her so intently that she burst out laughing.

"Oh, honestly! I'm fine, really! I just had the 'creeps' in the lighthouse, what with all the strange noises and things. Then an owl screeched right over my head and scared me out of my wits. So, I couldn't get to sleep. There's no electricity or water—I used my camping gear, and oh, I just wished all night long that I was back here with you. I heard all kinds of horrible noises, sort of like screams and crying, but—really, I'm fine. Sophie, that lasagna was the best present I ever had and you're all so sweet and thoughtful to me." Her words rambled and ran together as tears welled up in her eyes and she came to the realization of just how miserable she was without the comforts of home. She knew her reaction was out of nerves and lack of sleep, but she just wanted to cry herself unconscious. She had to guard her tongue, careful not to let anything about the caves or meeting with Jim Strongheart gush out until she'd figured out what was going on underneath her new home.

"Oh, gosh, I'm so sorry. I'm just tired. Really." She sobbed, trying to muster a reassuring smile to ease her new friends' stricken faces.

"Now, honey, don't go getting' all soggy on us. I tell you what, Joe Donelly's over at Beachfront Bed & Breakfast," Otis said, patting Mikela's hand. "I'll run over there right now and we'll git him over to the lighthouse to hook up your electric. How's that sound? His weekend job is doin' the local handiwork around here and he'll fix your water and everything else you need done to get the place a little more civilized for ya, okay?" Otis cocked his head and tried his impish wink, wanting Mikela to meet his eyes and laugh. Like a lot of other men, seeing a woman cry was Otis' undoing.

"Everything'll be all right, dear," Sophie said. "You can call the phone company from the back room and set up your phone service from here. In a day or two, it'll be just like home." Sophie smiled warmly as Mikela dried her tears with a paper napkin. "Come on, follow me and bring your coffee."

Sophie pushed her chair back and waited for Mikela to do the same before walking through the swinging doors into the back room. Mikela smiled sheepishly at Ross, whose intense gray eyes never left hers. She was not in the habit of losing control of her emotions like this and she could feel the warmth of embarrassment spreading across her cheeks. She followed Sophie past several refrigerators and freezers, a stainless steel work table and sinks built against one wall. Taking a corner to the left, the kitchen area disappeared behind them, replaced by a long, rectangular room, its main occupant an overstuffed, well-used couch. A lamp stand stood at the far end of the couch, the faded lampshade making a soft light all around the room. There were a couple of phone books stacked underneath an old-fashioned heavy, black telephone. A small television set was sitting lop-sided on two overturned milk crates facing the couch, its "rabbit ears" antennae covered with tin foil on the ends. Nestled between the comfy-looking couch and the little television set was a battered old coffee table with a few magazines scattered on it and a scented candle burning in the center.

"Here, Mikela." Sophie said as she sat Mikela down and put the phone books in her lap. With nimble fingers she opened up the phone book and quickly found the telephone company's number. "After you've got your arrangements made, you let me know what time to wake you, and you go to sleep for awhile. Nobody'll bother you back here."

"Oh, Sophie, thank you so much." Mikela managed, trying not to get choked up at Sophie's kindness. "I don't know what I'd do without you."

"Get yourself all moved in so I can come and see that lighthouse of yours! That'll be thanks enough, honey," Sophie smiled and patted the younger woman's shoulder. "Now go and make your call. Otis will take care of the rest and I'll wake you up in a little while." Sophie turned on her heel and walked away. Mikela could hear Otis, Ross and Sophie's murmurs like soft background music as she dialed the numbers to the phone company. She smiled to herself, grateful for the wonderful new friends she was making.

Having given information needed to install her phone service at the lighthouse, Mikela couldn't help but slide her body to a horizontal position on the couch, using the puffy armrest as a pillow. She kicked off her shoes, sliding them underneath the coffee table with a dangling foot, not wanting to be a messy guest. She would just close her eyes for a few minutes and then be on her way.

"Mikela...Mikela." A deep, soothing voice cooed. She struggled to open one eye from just having fallen into a deep sleep. "Here's your purse. I have to go back to work, but wanted to say goodbye." Ross knelt by the side of the couch. He brushed the hair from Mikela's face with his hand. "I'll stop by in a couple of hours to see how you're doing and maybe we'll have some dinner, okay?"

Mikela mumbled something incoherent, lost in the dream she was having, and drifted back to sleep.

Chapter Nine

Mikela awoke at 3:00 p.m. to the news that Joe Donelly, the handy-man, would meet her at the lighthouse in half an hour. After giving hurried "thank you" hugs to Sophie and Otis and making herself a "to-go" cup of coffee, she dashed out of the store and quickly drove to the lighthouse. She'd gotten about eight hours of sleep and felt so much better than when she'd come to town that morning. She barely remembered a couple of crazy dreams she'd had, but they both involved Jim Strongheart. She didn't know what to make of her last meeting with him and needed some time alone to think things through. Once she was in the lighthouse and could do normal, everyday things like taking a shower and making coffee, she was sure she'd be back to her old self.

A disheveled Joe Donelly was standing outside his pickup truck as Mikela pulled up to the lighthouse door. Dressed in jeans and flannel, a bit scruffy-looking with a day's growth of beard, he had dark graying hair, a bit of a beer belly and watery blue eyes. He stuck out his hand and Mikela took it, giving him a firm handshake. "I always wanted to see the inside of this place," he smiled. "What do you need besides the water turned on? Otis already had me turn on your electricity. I could do that from outside."

Mikela pushed the door open and led the way into the center of the big main room. "Well, Joe, the water's the main thing. The bathroom was winterized about ten years ago, so I need to make sure the shower and toilet will work. I want to be able to use the fireplace, but I have no idea the last time anyone's cleaned the chimney. And then there's…" Mikela rummaged through her purse and pulled out a notebook. Scanning it, she rattled off a list of repairs she'd noted earlier and ended with, "There are probably a lot of other things that need repair I haven't discovered yet." As they walked through the rooms, Mikela pointed out repairs needed from the notes she made. She told him of future renovations she'd like to do as well. "Oh, this is great! Now I can get the place cleaned up as soon as I have running water—can you check on the water heater, too?"

Joe was nodding his head. "Otis told me to take special care of you, Miss Williams, so I'll get to everything just as fast as I can. We'll work on the water first and go down the list. It'll probably be a week or two before I can get to the beacon and see what we can do up there."

After locating the water heater, Joe went outside to get his tool box. Mikela decided that while he was working in the house, she'd walk along the bluff and find the path she'd taken to walk down to the beach the day before. With any luck she'd run into Jim. She left Joe working in the bathroom, tools scattered around him on the floor, taking a metal plate off the base of the water heater. She retraced steps of the previous night and walked through the copse of pines to the edge of the bluffs that looked out over the Atlantic Ocean. The beginnings of a beautiful sunset greeted her when she stood on the bluff's edge, feeling like the only human on the island. The sound of the breaking waves coupled with the glorious view worked their magic on Mikela. The sun was making an orange path from the edge of the world right to where she was standing. For just a moment she felt invincible, yet vunerable at the same time, like she was standing on the edge of a new adventure. She welcomed the uncertainty that lay ahead and knew all her questions would be answered in time. Breathing in the scent of the briney water, feeling the same pull of the ocean that must have called to the natives that lived there long before, Mikela felt peace all around her. She knew then she'd made the right decision, leaving the world behind to find solace and a new life.

The call of a lonely tern broke through Mikela's reverie and she reluctantly turned from her dreamlike thoughts to retrace her steps and see what progress Joe had made in the lighthouse. She didn't realize it, but she'd been standing at the edge of the bluff for almost an hour. As she turned, Mikela's heart skipped a beat and she broke into a broad smile as she saw light coming from the little windows and glowing from the beacon tower at the top of lighthouse. "Yes!" she exclaimed, punching the air and quickening her step, excited to be able to see progress being made.

"I sure hope that smile's for me," a familiar voice came from the shadows and caused Mikela to stop dead in her tracks. The lighthouse door stood open, the man facing her only a black silhouette against the light radiating from the entry. For just a moment she thought it was Jim. She forced back her disappoint at the realization that Ross stood before her.

"Oh, Ross. Hello. I wasn't expecting you," Mikela offered, resuming her stride.

"I was hoping you'd be glad to see me. You must have forgotten my offer of dinner tonight." Ross wasn't in his uniform this time. He was long and lean in jeans and a button up shirt, sleeves rolled to his forearms, leather cowboy boots on his feet. As Mikela neared the door, he came into focus and they walked down the steps into the main room together.

"Ross…I'm..uh, sorry," Mikela stammered. "I really don't remember making any plans." Mikela felt heat on her cheeks as she remembered her crying and babbling that morning.

Ross turned to face her, stroking her hair with one hand. The intimate gesture made Mikela a bit uneasy. "Well, you need to eat and so do I. We'll just get something quick and I'll bring you right back home so you can call it an early night. You know, I've been waiting all day for this. I hope you like seafood." Ross made a sad 'puppy dog' face and Mikela couldn't help but laugh.

"Oh, Ross, I just got back a little while ago and haven't even had a shower yet. My hair's a mess, no makeup. I don't know how much longer Joe will be here…" Ross put his fingers to Mikela's lips in an effort to silence her protests.

"I've already talked with Joe. He's done for the day and will be leaving in a few minutes. He said he's got things in good shape." As if on cue, Joe walked out of the kitchen, toolbox in hand, as Ross was telling Mikela the news.

"I see you've already met the local law, Miss Williams," smiled Joe. "Your kitchen and bathroom are working fine. I let the water run while you were out. It was pretty rusty, but seems to be runnin' clear now. I'll be back tomorrow after work and see about the chimney and whatever else you want done then." He walked up the steps, nodding to Ross and Mikela and disappeared into the dark. Mikela heard his truck door open and then close, followed by the sound of the engine being started and the truck moving away as Joe went home for the night.

"So how long will it take you to get ready?" asked Ross. "I'm starving!"

"Are you positive you don't want a raincheck? Even a quick shower will take me at least a half an hour. Probably closer to an hour."

"No. Absolutely not. You take your shower and do what you have to do. I'll check this place out for you while you're doing your girly stuff." Ross' smile was pleasant but firm as he assumed a take-charge air. Mikela realized that she was famished and agreed to dinner. It would probably be a good idea to have a little chat with Ross. He was already walking toward the stairway that ran along the inside wall leading to the upstairs levels. She knew she'd explained to him that she wanted to be alone for a few days, but maybe this way he'd be out of her hair while she showered and dressed. She wasn't crazy about a strange man lurking outside her door while she was naked and defenseless in the bathroom, even if he was the law!

"Ok, then, if you don't mind waiting. I'll be as quick as I can." She smiled up at Ross, warming to the thought of having dinner with him, but he'd already started up the stairs. She fished through her duffel bag, located a towel and her toiletries bag and set her shampoo and soap on the shelf in the shower after quickly rinsing out the cobwebs. The next task was finding a pair of jeans and a decent shirt to wear to dinner. All the clothes she'd brought had been in her duffel bag for the last few days and were badly wrinkled. Maybe the steam from the shower would help make her a little more presentable. She slid the lock. Yes, although she'd much rather be sitting across a table from Jim Strongheart and staring into those smoldering eyes, this dinner with Ross would be a good thing. She could find out if he knew about the history of the lighthouse and maybe pick up a few pointers to help her in her sleuthing about what was going on in those caves at the same time…besides, she mused, a single girl can never have too many friends.

The water heater hadn't had enough time to do its job, so Mikela hurriedly washed and rinsed her hair and body in the spray of cool water. *At least it wasn't icy cold*, she thought. She toweled off and dressed, hoping Ross wouldn't be too embarrassed by her wrinkled clothes if they ran into any of his friends. She turned on the blow dryer, thinking about Ross as she finished getting ready. She had never seen him with a wrinkle, a scuff mark, a hair out of place. His nails were immaculate, manners impeccable. She wondered why she wasn't more attracted to him, but she just couldn't find a way to compare the two men that seemed to occupy her thoughts lately. Ross was rigid and perfect, probably a pillar-of-the-community type of guy while Jim was casual, more at ease in the natural world. The attraction to Jim was genuine and strong, and even though she barely knew him, he had a very real place in her heart. She silently prayed that Jim was safe and would come to her soon and explain what, exactly, was going on in the caverns below. She turned off the blow dryer and pulled a few cosmetics out of her bag. She lightly brushed some blush on her cheeks and applied mascara to her lashes. A little lip gloss and she was ready.

She came out of the bathroom and dropped her duffel bag and laundry on top of her makeshift bed. She seemed to be alone. "Ross?" she called. Not hearing a reply, she looked into the kitchen but he wasn't there. Through the kitchen window, she thought she spotted something moving along the edge of the bluff and turned off the kitchen light to get a better look. At the edge of the bluff, fully silhouetted by the great oval of moon rising from the ocean, were two wolves. Mikela smiled, remembering Abby and Niska, wondering if maybe Jim wasn't nearby and would come to her tonight. She smiled at the thought. She'd have to ask Ross if wolves were native to Beam Island. She called his name again, wondering where he'd gone. Walking into the bedroom, she saw a light coming from the closet door. She flipped the switch on the bedroom wall.

"Ross, I'm ready," she called. "Ross?" She pushed the closet door open farther and could see an opening large enough for a person to crouch down and pass through. She followed the light, passing through the closet into another room that apparently was used at one time for storage, since it had shelves along one side. It went back about six more feet and there was a large square of light coming up from underneath the floor. A heavy-looking wooden hatch was propped against the wall. Mikela slowly and cautiously peered over the edge and saw several rung-like steps leading down underneath the foundation of the lighthouse. "Ross?" she called. "Are you there?" She heard some shuffling noises, then the top of Ross' head emerged, followed by the rest of his body as he climbed back into the hidden room.

"This is some place you've got here, Mikela. I hope you don't mind that I did a little exploring while you were getting ready." It was more a statement than a question. Mikela backed out of the passageway, made her way back into the closet area and finally, into the bedroom. She heard a loud thud as Ross laid the heavy hatch back down. A few seconds later, he stepped into the bedroom, brushing cobwebs from his clothes and hands.

"It'll just take me a minute to wash up before we leave."

Mikela followed Ross from the bedroom to the bathroom, leaning in the doorway as she spoke. "Ross, what were you doing? I thought you were just going upstairs. What if you had fallen down that shaft and I couldn't find you?" Mikela was trying to recover her composure. She was angry that he'd been snooping around her new home and discovering something that should have been hers to discover. Wondering what other liberties he'd taken in her house while she was locked in the shower, she tried to calm herself. Ross looked at her and smiled easily as he took a comb from his back pocket and pulled it through his short hair a few times.

"I tried to ask you if you'd mind, but you had the bathroom door locked and you wouldn't have heard me. I'm sorry, Mikela, I didn't mean to do anything to upset you." He put his comb away and reached for her arms, but she turned and walked into the main room.

"It's all right, Ross. I'm probably over-reacting. I haven't been my-self the last few days. I just wanted to be here alone while I got the place set up and livable, rehash my memories, stuff like that. I'm a wrinkled mess and can't offer you a drink or anything. I'm afraid I'm not on my best hostess behavior. And now you're discovering some strange things about my new home that I would have liked to been in on, that's all." Mikela made a face at Ross and then smiled. "I'm sorry."

"No problem. You're a woman. I guess you're supposed to worry about your clothes, but there's no need to. This is a tourist town. People dress more for comfort than for style, Mikela. Come on, let's go." Ross took Mikela's elbow and they walked to the door. "Still mad at me?" he smiled.

"No, of course not, Ross," she returned his smile with her lips but it didn't reach her eyes. She was certain what was bothering her was Ross' attitude, not her worry about clothes! She hadn't noticed his vehicle when she first saw him earlier in the evening when he'd parked on the other side of Joe Donelly's truck and was surprised at the silver Corvette that met her gaze.

"Wow," was all she managed to say. Ross came around the passenger's side of the car and held her door open for her. "Now I really feel underdressed." She slid down in the low bucket seat as Ross shut her door. He came around and slid behind the wheel.

"I've had a thing for fast cars ever since I can remember," Ross told her. "I've restored several of them. I'm glad to see you appreciate her." He caressed the dashboard as he told Mikela some impressive names of other vehicles he'd restored. She nodded at the appropriate time and tried to appear interested in his small talk but it looked like the en-tire evening was going to be a one-sided conversation. Her mind drifted back to the picture of Ross climbing out of the mysterious shaft in her bedroom closet and the memory of his telling her the bathroom door had been locked! He'd been climbing up the stairs to the tower when she'd slid the bolt—did he actually try the door to see if it was unlocked? If Mikela wasn't so determined to discover what Jim was up to, she'd make up some excuse about a pounding headache just to get out of this evening's dinner.

In a few moments, Mikela realized that Ross had taken her to the resort area of the island. The larger marinas boasted some very elegant restaurants, but his car continued down the road toward the jetty that was surrounded by fishing vessels, mostly lobster boats. The parking lot was a maze of pickup trucks and utility vehicles, obviously a popular spot among the locals. A nondescript wooden structure, The Fish Tale had brightly glowing neon beer signs hanging in each of its many windows and featured a wrap-around deck that had a dozen or more picnic tables scattered about, their umbrellas folded up this time of year.

After parking his car diagonally across two parking spaces, Ross jumped out of the Corvette and hurried to the passenger side, opening the door for Mikela. They climbed the few stairs to the restaurant's entrance and Ross pulled the door open at the same time putting his arm posses-sively around Mikela as they walked in together. Mikela fought the urge to pull away, not wanting to embarrass Ross in front of the many faces he was nodding to. A young woman with spiked, bright red hair showed them to a comfortable booth. Mikela noted that the waitress seemed to have a penchant for dog collars and tattoos as she paraded herself from behind the bar with a tray that held two glasses of water. She set down the glasses, dropped the menus on the table, rattled off the day's specials and flirted for a moment with Ross, winking at him after taking their drink orders. Ross winked back and then looked at Mikela who was frowning at him.

"Oh, Joni's just a kid, Mikela, don't look so serious. Unfortunately, she's a regular bust for me, so she's not someone I'd want to introduce you to," he laughed. Whether at a memory or maybe at the look on her face, Mikela wasn't sure, but she busied herself with the menu. She would be so happy when this evening was over.

"I didn't realize I was, Ross. I guess I'm still not quite myself. So what's good on the menu? Everything sounds wonderful!" She forced a smile as she read the plastic coated pages she held in both hands.

Ross covered one of Mikela's hands with his own. "Why don't you let me order for both of us and I'll surprise you?" He patted her hand and held it for just a minute. She smiled and then looked around the room. She felt awkward and tried to make small talk, feeling that Ross was trying to force affection on her that she didn't want. In a few moments, Joni was back at their table with frosty mugs of beer and bowls of clam chowder. They seemed to be on the 'family' side of the restaurant. Couples with children were sitting at the booths on this side of the room. Beyond the old brass-railed bar, complete with a mirrored back wall that reflected rows of various brands of liquors, were pool tables. She could hear the clack of the balls as they hit each other, plunked into the pockets and then rolled to their final resting place. An occasional loud voice would rise above the others, followed by raucous laughter. The smell of cigarettes filled the air. It was a typical New England workingman's bar and the kind of place that Mikela and her girlfriends, when first old enough to drink, would frequent on a Saturday night. She smiled at The Fish Tale's typical Yankee décor. Fishing nets decorated the walls tied with colored glass floats and nautical decorations. There were several impressive, though dusty, mounted fish adorning the doorways.

Mikela looked around for the restrooms and made a mental note that they must be located toward the rear of the building. The area where Ross and Mikela were seated had a lattice wood wall that separated the dining room from the bar area, woven with nautical decorations and live plants, so Mikela could watch the comings and goings of the front door unobserved from her seat. Their table had a large window and Mikela's attention turned to the vehicles she could see in the parking lot. Any one of the dark pickup trucks with a camper shell could have been Jim's truck. She saw a weathered, wooden fence. Rough sea grasses tufted at the foot of the fence posts standing precariously at the crest of a dune. She saw that the moon had risen in the evening sky and remembered seeing the wolves earlier from her kitchen window.

"Ross," she asked, in between glorious swallows of thick, hot chowder, "Tell me about the wolves on Beam Island."

Ross put his spoon down and swallowed hard, looking at her quizzically. "Wolves? Where'd you get the idea that we had any wolves on the island? Unless you're talking about the two-legged kind." Joni must have thought Ross' comment was pretty funny because she giggled a lot louder than Mikela thought was necessary as she set their heaping plates of steamers and lobsters in front of them.

Chapter Ten

Mikela tried her best to keep focused on Ross' conversation, but now her thoughts were almost exclusively of Jim. The wolves she saw in the moonlight must have been Niska and Abby, so Jim had to be near the lighthouse. Were the dogs waiting for their master to come from the caves? Was Jim in danger? She had to find out about the caves.

"Ross, this is really great! The food is fabulous." She smiled up at him, trying her best to flirt. "You were right that I needed to eat. And while you're feeding me, tell me more about the island." She dunked another fat steamer into a bowl of broth, then dipped it into clarified butter. These were truly the best steamers she'd ever eaten. She reached for another one and said casually, "How about the legend of the caves? Do you think the passageway in the lighthouse might be connected to them? Or is it just a legend?" she asked as she popped another buttery steamer into her mouth.

The front door banged open and a group of men walked into The Fish Tale. The two in front appeared to be dragging their feet and Mikela stole a sideways glance to look at the commotion. She almost choked on her food. It was Jim! She saw that one of the men held an object against Jim's spine. Could it be a gun? Or maybe a knife? She couldn't see Jim's face to know if he was there with his friends or someone was forcing him into the bar, but he didn't look too happy.

Ross followed Mikela's eyes with his own and took in the motley looking group. "You want to keep clear of them, Mikela. They're in the same league as Joni. Most of them, anyway. Looks like there are a couple of new ones I haven't had the pleasure of meeting yet. But it's only a matter of time," Ross shook his head as he tore a lobster claw loose and worked on cracking it open. "But back to your question. There are a lot of different versions of the cave stories. The original is that they're haunted by the ghosts of Indian women, mothers and brides who lost their men to white smugglers in the late 1800s. And it's true that you can hear a wailing sound when the tide's going out, because I've heard it myself. No one's ever been able to map the caves. Some of the caverns are so small and narrow that a man can't fit in them, but the main reason is that the only way in is from the beach and when the tide is high, the entrance disappears and it creates a riptide, so you can't scuba dive in there. I thought I'd found another way inside the caves tonight from your light-house, but the shaft narrowed from the ladder. Maybe it was to hide the lighthouse keeper in a storm or from attacking smugglers or something. I couldn't get much further down than 15, maybe 20 feet. With all the spiders and creepy crawlers down there, I doubt you'll want to open it again, anyway. Don't worry about those bugs getting into the bedroom, though. I've got that passageway shut up tighter than Fort Knox. Nothing will crawl through it."

Mikela smiled and nodded, only half listening to what Ross was saying, although when he got to the part about the passageway, her ears pricked up. She wondered why he was trying so hard to scare her away from going near it. Mikela wasn't sure what she should do. She wanted to get a better look at the man she thought was Jim. Maybe her imagination was playing tricks on her—after all, it was dimly lit in the restaurant. If it was Jim, she owed it to him to see if he needed her help. She knew something dangerous was going on underneath the island, but she didn't know if she should involve Ross or not. Maybe she could see what was happening if she could get closer to the bar. Joni just delivered another round of beers, so Mikela asked her where to find the ladies room. Joni pointed past the bar, right where Jim and the other men had been heading. Joni giggled and told Mikela not to worry, she'd keep Ross occupied while she was gone and slid into Mikela's seat. Ross laughed and almost choked on his beer.

"Yes… I'm sure you will," Mikela said stiffly.

She clutched her purse tightly to her body and headed in the direction of the restroom, walking slowly and scanning the dark corners searching for Jim in the shadows. He wasn't in the groups gathered around the pool tables or sitting at the bar. At the far end of the bar was a sign hanging from the ceiling that read "Restrooms" with an arrow pointing beneath it. Mikela saw several doors; an exit directly at the end of the hallway, a door marked "Mates" and another marked "Maids." She fought the urge to roll her eyes. Unless Jim had gone to the kitchen or out the back door exit, she didn't know where else to look. She'd try and think of an excuse to get into the kitchen while pretending to use the bathroom. She turned the handle and found it locked. While waiting, she noticed that the men's room wasn't completely shut, so it was probably empty. That eliminated one room.

She heard a toilet flush, followed by the sound of water running in a sink. The water stopped and an automatic hand dryer started. A few seconds later she heard the lock click and the door opened. The girl coming out of the restroom smiled at Mikela on her way out, turning sideways to pass in the narrow hallway. Mikela stepped into the small bathroom and tried to think of what to do. If Jim got too far away, she'd never be able to find him. But if he were here in this building, then she needed to find him fast. She heard a muffled thud coming from behind the bathroom wall. She looked up into the stall and saw some sort of heating or air vent. She made sure the door was securely locked and set her purse on the sink. She needed something to stand on, to see if she could see or hear anything from the vent. With nothing to climb on in the tiny bathroom, Mikela stepped up onto the toilet seat and stood carefully on its sides. She grabbed the side of the stall for balance and stood on her tiptoes. It was a heating vent that opened into the kitchen on the other side and, if she squinted just right she could look straight through the slats! What she saw caused her heart to sink.

Slumped in the corner of the kitchen, near another rear exit, Mikela saw Jim and another man. Their wrists were tied and both were bleeding from head wounds. It looked like they were leaning against each other for support. She gasped as she saw Jim take a painful punch to the ribs. He slid in a heap to the floor, taking his buddy with him. As she watched in horror, two more men, whose voices she recognized from the caves, came into her line of vision. She strained to hear what they were saying.

"Just leave these bastids here for now so they can't get away. At closin', toss 'em out the back door by the trash cans. Tell Joni to go on home early tonight, I don't want her gettin' in the way. We'll drop these two pieces o' shit off the bluffs at the lighthouse before daybreak. It won't take but 20 minutes and they'll be history. Leave 'em trussed, too. I don't want a chance they'll be able to swim away or grab onto a rock or somethin'." The man doing all the talking had his back to her, but Mikela heard every chilling syllable, perfectly clear. "By tomorrow, these bastids won't be nuthin' but a bad memory."

A fit of coughing drowned out the rest of his words. Mikela flinched as the man doing all the talking kicked Jim hard in the side. Someone knocked on the bathroom door just then and Mikela's heart pounded in her chest. Had she been discovered? She jumped backward off the toilet seat and wiped any possible footprints from the seat. She flushed and called out, "Just a minute!" She ran the water and pushed the button to start the dryer, her heart beating furiously as she stalled for time, trying to formulate a plan.

What on earth could she do to save Jim? How could Ross know these people so well and not have a clue as to what they were up to? Or did he? She had to come up with a plan and quickly, as it was already 9:30 p.m. She'd have to find out how late the bar stayed open tonight. As much as she wanted to confide in Ross, her woman's intuition told her not to. There was just something about him she wasn't comfortable with and her instincts had saved her more than once in the past. When she got back home she'd have to find Abby and Niska and bring them back in the SUV. She would park out on the jetty with the dogs and find Jim. Together, they would bring him home.

Another knock sounded on the door. Mikela slid the bolt and grabbed her purse, murmuring a "sorry" as she left, almost knocking Joni over as she sped down the hallway. Joni stood in the doorway, staring after her, hands on her hips. Mikela came around through the pool room, passed the bar and looked up to see Ross already standing by their booth, waiting for her. She'd been wondering how to get him to quickly end the meal and take her home, but it looked as if he was ready to leave now.

"Sorry, Mikela," he said, "I got called back to work tonight. I'm going to have to drop you off and run. There's an accident with injuries on the causeway." They literally ran at a trot down the steps and through the parking lot. He had the doors open and the car running in a couple of seconds. "That's the downside of dating a trooper, we're always on call. I hope you can handle it."

Mikela assured Ross that there was no problem, she understood that 'duty called' and all that. She thanked him for the delicious dinner and told him that next time it would be her turn to buy.

"Now I don't mind if you cook for me, but I don't let a lady buy my dinner, Mikela," Ross said sternly. They'd pulled up in front of the lighthouse and Mikela took her key out, hoping she'd be able to get inside. Now was not the time for a talk about the state of their relationship or his chauvinistic attitude! Mikela glanced around, hoping for some sign of the dogs. Ross misinterpreted her searching gaze for uncertainty and insisted on making sure Mikela was safely inside the structure before he left. He opened the door and gave Mikela a quick peck on the cheek before turning and saying, "I was hoping to give you a more memorable impression of me, but I guess I'll have to give you a raincheck. I'll see you in a couple of days." And with that, Ross turned on his heel, climbed into his car and disappeared in a cloud of dust, eerily illuminated in the red tail lights of the Corvette.

Mikela watched until she couldn't see the red lights anymore. When she was certain he was gone, she walked around to the bluff side of the lighthouse, searching for the dogs. The moon was high in the sky, not the giant illuminating ball it had been earlier. She walked to where she was certain they'd been sitting and called out their names. She was fairly certain Abby would come to her. Surely they knew her scent and that she was no danger to their master! She suddenly remembered the whistle Jim had used to call Abby the night she stayed at this house. It was two quick whistles. Mikela lamented the fact that she'd never really learned to whistle and was trying to make up for it now. She puckered and blew hard, twice. After several tries, she finally made a sound, and in a few minutes she knew that if the dogs were within earshot, they would come. She unlocked the SUV's doors and checked the items in her first aid kit. She opened the back of the vehicle, deciding that she'd better bring her sleeping bag and a blanket. She whistled again as she went into the house for the items she needed. "Abby! Here, girl! Nis-ka!"

The wind started to pick up and Mikela was afraid that her cries and whistles were being taken far out to sea, where no one would hear. She gathered her sleeping bag and an extra blanket, laying them in the back end of the SUV. She whistled a couple more times, grabbed some bottled water and a box of crackers. Abby and Niska were nowhere in sight. She thought she was ready to go when she remembered that she might need a flashlight and maybe a knife to cut through the ropes that bound Jim and the other man. She stopped long enough to call out the dogs' names and whistle one final time before going back into the lighthouse for the remaining items she thought might be needed tonight. Her heart sank as she realized she'd be going back to The Fish Tale alone. A couple of days before, Jim had saved her from the fury of the storm, and now she had to save him from the fury of those men at the bar. Her heart pumping with adrenaline, her mind racing to form a foolproof plan to help Jim, she shut the lighthouse door behind her and practically ran to the SUV. As she opened the door to get in, she was pushed aside as two huge and breathless bundles of fur leapt past her and into the vehicle. Each bounced from the passenger seat to the back seat, their tongues hanging low, sides heaving, gasping for breath.

"Thank God!" Mikela cried, overjoyed. She turned around and knelt in the driver's seat, reaching behind to hug the dogs' necks. "I *knew* you'd come and help me! Oh, Abby, it's so good to see you! Niska!" She buried her face in their furry necks, hugging them furiously. They responded with sloppy kisses, tails wagging back and forth in a frenzy. With the two dogs by her side, Mikela's fears melted away. Together, they would find Jim. She straightened up, turning back around in her seat.

Wiping the dogs' kisses off her face with the back of her sleeve, she turned the key in the ignition, fastened her seat belt, and shifted into *drive*. "Okay, you two. Let's go find your daddy."

Chapter Eleven

Mikela drove slowly past the marinas, retracing her earlier ride with Ross. She headed toward the jetty, scouting the area for a parking spot where she could be well hidden and yet have a good view of The Fish Tale and its parking area. She kept up a constant commentary with the dogs. It was comforting to talk to them even if they couldn't answer her. "This looks like a good spot, sort of hidden behind these lobster traps. We need to keep an eye on the back door, because that's where those thugs are going to toss your dad and his buddy at closing time. See that dumpster? I think that's where we'll find them…keep your eyes peeled…it's a little after 11…how much longer can they stay open? Maybe when this is over, you two could put in a good word for me. Your dad and I have some unfinished business. He drives me nuts, you know, but I just can't stop thinking about him…"

Her last words hung in the air. Mikela's heart skipped a beat when she saw the back door of the restaurant open wide. Niska and Abby sat up at the sound of the door opening, all senses alert. Niska sniffed the air for clues. A skinny man wearing a once-white chef's apron emerged from the light of the open door. He carried a big black garbage bag in each hand and Mikela could see the red glow of a cigarette hanging from his mouth. He walked to the front of the dumpster, dropped both bags on the ground and leaned back against the side of the metal container, obviously in no hurry, intent on enjoying his cigarette.

From the front door, Mikela watched as customers began exiting in groups of twos and threes, the occasional straggler coming out alone.

Last call must have been sounded from the bar, so she guessed closing time must be 11:30 p.m. or midnight. The front door opened again and Joni pranced down the front steps pulling on what looked like a satin letter jacket. She stopped in her tracks, shouting something over her shoulder and stood waiting. A few seconds later, one of the men Mikela had seen playing pool caught up with the flirty waitress and put his arm around her shoulders. Big and mean-looking, he bent his shaggy dark head down under Joni's spiked red hair and it looked like Joni's evening entertainment had begun.

Mikela's gaze wandered over to the man taking a cigarette break at the dumpster. He was making hand gestures to someone standing inside the back door. Finally he threw both hands in the air, then tossed his cigarette on the ground and angrily stomped it out. He lifted the cover from one side of the dumpster, dropped in the two trash bags, and slammed the lid back down. He stomped back up the stairs and slammed the door behind him.

"Did you see anyone that looked like your dad, Abby? It looks like the bar's almost empty…probably just the kitchen help are left…I'm sure they're in a hurry to go home, so maybe we won't have long to wait."

Mikela was babbling to Abby and Niska again. She noticed that the inside of the SUV was fogging up from their breath, but she didn't want to take a chance of turning on the engine and drawing attention their way.

She had parked on an angle from the restaurant's back door, partially hidden by a pile of old wooden lobster traps. The owner of the vehicle closest to her had gotten into his pickup truck and driven away, not even looking in her direction, so she felt pretty safe. Their twenty minute wait seemed like hours.

The dogs had just settled down in the rear seat when Mikela saw that the back door to the restaurant was opening. Once again, Niska and Abby sat at attention, sniffing the air, listening with ears erect. The men walked slowly out of the back door, one walking toward the parking lot, the other lost in the shadows on the side where the ocean stretched out like black ink. In a moment, they had circled back around and met by the dumpster, stopping to talk for a moment. She saw the flame from a match flicker and then die, replaced by two red glowing dots. Each had lit a cigarette and must have been making sure that all of this evening's customers had gone home.

Satisfied they were unobserved, they threw down their cigarettes, looked around a final time, and went back up the steps into the open doorway. This time only one man disappeared inside. The other bent down and leaned in. Mikela rubbed a spot of fog from the windshield. She could see the man outside had grabbed two legs, one boot under each arm, and was lifting upward—the other man had grabbed the motionless arms and together they were half-dragging, half-carrying the unconscious man down the steps. Together they swung the body back and forth several times and finally let him fly, only to land with a dull thud in a heap next to the scattered trash that hadn't made it into the dumpster. Mikela felt her stomach turn. Tears welled up in her eyes as she thought of how hurt and battered Jim and his friend might be. She prayed that Jim would be safe until she could get to him. Niksa started to make a low growl deep in his throat as Abby softly whimpered. They watched the same scene replayed as the second unconscious body was thrown from the back steps of the restaurant, landing with a sickening thud on top of the first body.

"Easy, Niska. Good girl, Abby. After Jim's safe, I'll bring you both back here and let you tear them apart if you want to, but for now we need to keep quiet. Shhh…"

The men stopped to light cigarettes yet again. Mikela was sure they were small time hoodlums, carrying out orders from a higher-up, they way they fidgeted and smoked. She watched aghast as one of the men flicked his still-burning cigarette onto the unmoving heap. His buddy had walked to the back door, closed and locked it, and together they came back down the steps. Niska let out a "woof" and stood on his haunches. Mikela saw the hair on the dog's back stand straight up and a deep, low growl rose out of his throat. The two men separated at the parking lot, one climbing on a motorcycle and the other into a rusty car. She felt the rumble from their mufflers as they sped away from the marina.

Her knuckles gripped the steering wheel so hard, they turned white.

It hurt her to sit and watch and not be able to do anything to help Jim. Her thoughts went back to the man who had saved her from the storm, made her coffee and kissed her so passionately. The tears silently slid down her cheeks, blurring her vision. Abby wriggled her way into the front seat and put her head down on Mikela's shoulder, whimpering softly. The three waited a full five minutes before daring to start the SUV. She wiped the fog from the inside of the windshield, sent up a silent prayer and turned the key in the ignition. She put the defogger on full blast and let the vehicle idle for a moment as she peered through the night to see if anyone was about. Her headlights illuminated the area where the two bodies had been tossed. Nothing was moving. She pulled out from behind the cover of the pile of lobster traps and drove slowly to the right, sweeping the restaurant and the dumpster area with her headlights. She continued onto the pier and turned the vehicle around slowly, carefully watching for any movement or other headlights. She saw nothing.

She pulled up alongside the dumpster. "Okay, let's go." She opened her door and slid to the ground—Abby and Niska bounded past her. She crept around the rear of the SUV and ran to the bodies. "Jim! Jim!" she cried, kneeling next to the men. Both dogs were licking their master's face, then Niska took a sleeve and tried to drag him toward the vehicle. Their efforts were greeted with moans of pain. Mikela blinked away grateful tears as she realized with a certainty that Jim wasn't dead—at least not yet. "Jim, we need to hurry. Please help me. I need to get you and your friend into my SUV. Jim! Please wake up!" With a burst of strength she didn't know she possessed, Mikela hefted the limp body partly onto her shoulder and both dragged and pulled him toward the running vehicle. She lay the back seats down as Abby jumped into the back, turned, and bit into a sleeve, tugging with all her might as Mikela pushed. Together they got Jim into the back of the SUV.

"Jim, I have to get your friend. I'll be right back. Honey, please try to wake up!" Niska leapt into the backseat and licked his master's face. Jim was starting to come around. Abby and Mikela ran back to the dumpster and tugged and pulled on the second man, dragging him as best they could. The adrenaline high Mikela felt surging through her body gave her the extra energy and strength she needed to finally get the second man into the vehicle, alongside Jim.

"Wake up. Please wake up…we're trying to help you!" she cried. The man was trying to move his legs, but couldn't quite gain consciousness. At last Mikela had both men inside the vehicle and could completely shut the doors. With Niska in the back guarding his master and companion, she opened the passenger door to let Abby in and hurried to the driver's side. She hopped up into the seat, pressed the 'lock' button on the console and heard the resounding *thunk* as all the door locks were secured. She shifted into *drive* and stepped on the gas, a lingering feeling of dread accompanying her as they drove away from the pier, The Fish Tale, and the marinas.

At the stop sign, Mikela looked in her rear view mirror to see if they were being followed. She saw no signs of life at all. Feeling less fearful, she headed toward home, trying to miss the potholes as they wound their way along the dirt road that led back through the island, meandered past the houses and through the wildlife refuge. After what seemed like an eternity, the SUV passed under the canopy of trees that opened onto her property and she saw the welcoming glow of light surrounding the top of the lighthouse like a halo.

"Oh, thank you, God! Jim, we're here! Abby, Niska, we made it!" Mikela's smile lit up her face. She didn't realize how tense she was until the adrenaline drained from her body. She pulled the SUV around with the passenger door facing the entrance to the lighthouse. Breathing a deep sigh of relief, she switched off the ignition and leaned her forehead against the steering wheel, taking a deep breath as she steeled herself to the task of moving the two battered men once again. Carrying them down should be much easier than trying to lift them up, she reasoned.

The male dog's deep, throaty growl brought Mikela to attention. Lifting up her head, her eyes riveted on the unwelcome sight of a pair of low-slung Corvette headlights bobbing up and down over the uneven sand surface of her driveway, coming closer and closer.

Chapter Twelve

"Oh, no…" Mikela groaned. "Jim! Jim, listen to me. You've got to stay quiet. Someone's coming up the driveway. Don't make a sound, either one of you!" She turned in her seat and unfolded the extra blanket she'd brought along, tossing one end toward the rear of the vehicle, trying to cover the two men. Niska carefully inched his way toward the front seats. Was he sensing danger up ahead? Thinking quickly, Mikela increased the volume on the radio. "Abby, come with me. Niska, stay." She commanded, as she opened her door and slid out of the driver's seat.

The Corvette rolled to a stop as Abby obediently climbed out of the vehicle and sat at Mikela's feet. Mikela shut the door, effectively extinguishing the interior light of the SUV, trying to block Ross' view. The interior went black just as Ross climbed out of his sports car. Satisfied that he hadn't seen any movement in her vehicle, Mikela walked over to greet Ross with Abby heeling at her side.

"Well, what are you doing here?" she asked, trying to sound pleasantly surprised. "I thought you had to work an accident." Ross looked at Mikela and then at Abby, his features unsmiling. "Where were you just now and where'd you get—that?" he demanded, nodding at Abby.

"Emm…she's my dog." Mikela lamely answered, patting Abby's head. "What's wrong, Ross?" she asked, shocked to see the anger he directed toward her.

"Answer the rest of my question, Mikela," he ordered, folding his arms across his chest, his eyes narrowed in a very unpleasant stare.

"Excuse me?" Mikela asked, incredulous. "Are you interrogating me?"

Her eyebrows shot up and hands went to hips in as defiant a posture as she could manage. The breeze picked up, whipping her hair around her head. She was glad of nature's help in drowning out any moans or noises that might be coming from the back of her vehicle.

"I leave you for an hour and you're out bar-hopping the minute my back is turned!" Ross angrily accused.

Mikela's mouth dropped open. She couldn't believe what she was hearing. Was this guy serious? "Ross, I think we've got a problem here. You and I had a couple of beers and almost one dinner together. I don't owe you any explanations for anything I do. In fact, I think you'd better leave." Mikela tried her best to feel brave, but her knees were shaking. Her intuition had warned her not to trust Ross and now she knew why. She nervously tucked a strand of hair behind her ear. Without a sound, Abby stood and moved closer to Ross, the hair on the back of her neck standing up straight, her body alert to danger. She didn't growl but positioned herself between the angry man and her friend.

At Mikela's open defiance, Ross backed down. "Listen, Mikela, I'm sorry. It's just the cop coming out in me," he said, trying to make light of his behavior. "We had some trouble down at the marina after I left and then I saw you driving back here. I was afraid that something had happened to you. I'm just concerned." His eyes moved to the dog and back up to Mikela's face. He took a tentative step toward her, but thought better of moving closer. He was getting visibly frustrated. "Mikela, why don't you invite me in so I can see for myself that everything's okay?" As an afterthought he added, "I never did get to really kiss you goodnight." He moved slowly toward her.

"What do you mean 'trouble at the marina'?" Mikela tried to change the subject. What did Ross know about the events that took place a few hours ago? He was supposed to have gone to the causeway toward the mainland. He must have lied about why he had to leave in the middle of dinner. She knew darn well Ross wasn't worried about her. There was something he wanted to see for himself in the lighthouse. He had snooped around earlier while she was in the shower and he was going to try and bully his way back inside the lighthouse now. Mikela took a step back. She didn't want him anywhere near her home.

"Nothing I can talk about right now, sweetheart. But you could be in danger out here all by yourself. I warned you back at the store about moving into this lighthouse, didn't I?" He switched to a patronizing tone as he took another step forward. "Come on, Mikela. Just one cup of coffee and I'll leave." Ross stepped close enough to touch her and put his hand on her forearm. "Come on, honey, be nice to Ross." He leaned in to kiss her and Mikela fell backward against the SUV, trying to avoid his kiss. She grabbed wildly for the driver's door handle as Ross put his hand around her waist, pulling her into a tight embrace. "Come on, baby," he whined. Ross caught Mikela and was pulling her toward him.

"Ross, let go of me! Let go!" Mikela screamed, punching at his chest while trying to kick and push him away. Abby in an instant, attacked with a viselike grip digging her teeth into the leather of Ross' boot, wildly shaking her head. Mikela's hand finally connected with the door handle and she pulled frantically, releasing the latch. Before he knew what happened, Ross was face to face with the bare fangs and claws of Niska. Niska leapt with all his strength onto a surprised Ross, pinning him to the ground, fangs threatening to tear out the throat of the state trooper. Ross quit fighting and lay perfectly still.

"Get-him-off-me-now."

Mikela stood up slowly, brushing the sand from her jeans, her heart still beating wildly. She realized that the door to the SUV was open and illuminating the inside of her vehicle, so she stole a quick glance inside. It didn't seem that the commotion outside had wakened its passengers. She quickly slammed the door closed, praying that Jim was only unconscious and not dead from his brutal beating.

"Unless you want real trouble, get this dog off me *now,* " Ross was talking between clenched teeth trying to force his way out of this predicament. This was obviously a trained attack dog. If he moved the wrong way, the dog would rip out his throat. "Mikela, please," he pleaded.

Trembling, she straightened her blouse and raked shaking fingers through her hair, taking several deep, calming breaths. She had always respected the law and was dumbfounded that a policeman would treat a woman this way. She was so shaken that she couldn't think of a likely command to give Niska to have him let go of Ross' throat. When she had regained some of her composure, she simply said, "Sit, Niska." To her surprise, Niska sat back on his haunches. Ross scrambled backward away from the dog.

"Get out of here. Now. Don't you ever come back, Ross." Mikela wiped her mouth with the back of her hand, trying to remove the sickening feel of him from her lips. Her stomach churned with the realization that she would probably have been raped if Niska and Abby hadn't been there to protect her.

Ross stood up and surveyed the damage to his boot. "I guess I don't have to worry about you out here by yourself, do I?" he grinned. "Come on, Mikela, lighten up. This is all a big misunderstanding. I'll give you a day or two to think things over and when you calm down, we'll have dinner again. No harm done, sweetheart." He stood looking at her for a moment. "I guess I won't bother trying to kiss you goodbye again." He turned on his heel and folded himself into the silver sports car. "Goodnight, Mikela." The engine turned over and he slowly drove down the path to the bluff road. Mikela stood open-mouthed, watching him leave. She stood and waited until his tail lights disappeared for the second time that evening, afraid to turn around until she was certain he was really gone.

She dropped to her knees and buried her face in her hands, sobbing. Abby and Niska rallied around her, nudging her with their noses. In each arm, she held onto one of the dogs and hugged them to her until her tears abated. She would deal with Ross later. Right now, she had to get Jim and the other man to safety and apparently, it wasn't safe here.

Chapter Thirteen

Mikela dried her tears and put her mind to work on the very real life or death situation she was in. She opened the back seat door and climbed up onto the makeshift bed. She carefully lifted the blanket she'd thrown over the two bodies and slowly pulled it off. The man lying closest to her was Jim. Still in a crumpled heap, he managed to touch Mikela's hand with his own. "I'm...so...sorry." Was all he could manage to whisper, followed by a low moan that broke Mikela's heart.

"Jim, is there anything I can do to make you more comfortable? I have no idea how badly beaten you are and your friend hasn't moved or said a word since I dragged him in here. I don't even know if he's still alive." Mikela had carefully climbed into the vehicle and was straddling over Jim's chest. She leaned close to his face and listened carefully, but nothing more came from his lips. It was difficult to imagine that those bruised and swollen lips were the same ones that had kissed her so passionately just twenty-four hours ago. "When this is all over, Jim Strongheart, don't you dare forget that I'm still waiting for you to come to me." Mikela searched his face and saw the corner of his mouth barely turn. He was trying to smile! "You'll be alright. Now I want you to hang in there, because we're going to find the hospital and get you and your friend all taken care of."

His hand moved to touch her wrist and he swallowed hard, not opening his eyes. "No. My house. My sister." The effort to speak proved too much and she could tell he'd slipped back into unconciousness. Mikela gently kissed his forehead and carefully backed out of the vehicle. She was on the verge of tears once more, wanting desperately for Jim to be healed.

She steeled herself to be strong. Opening the driver's door, she called to the dogs who immediately came and sat at her feet. "Let's go home!" she called and the two dogs jumped into the SUV. Niska gingerly climbed into the back and lay down between his master and the other man, while Abby sat upright in the passenger's seat, bright eyes peering forward into the darkness.

Mikela had left the radio running but now turned the volume down. Just enough sound to hear the news when it broadcast, hopefully to give her some idea of what had happened tonight in the caves and at the marina. She drove slowly down the sand path of her driveway and out onto the main road, her eyes continually sweeping the area lit by her headlights, alert for any signs of the silver Corvette. Jim wanted her to go to his house and contact his sister. She prayed that she was doing the right thing in not going to the nearest hospital or finding a phone booth and calling 9-1-1. She didn't know the physical state of either of the two men in the back, nor whether they were the "good guys" or the "bad guys." She would just have to follow her heart and her intuition and trust in herself. There was no one else to turn to. The only people she knew on the island were Sophie and Otis, and she'd met Ross at their store, so she had to assume they knew all about Ross. Well, she'd worry about them later. Right now, her goal was to get her cargo back to Jim's house. Once she got them safely inside his home and called his sister, then she'd figure out what to do from there. But she knew something would have to be done about Ross in the near future.

Mikela made it to the causeway without catching sight of Ross' Corvette. Her next worry was that the causeway would be blocked because of the accident, but she didn't see any flashing lights up ahead in the dark. In fact, there wasn't any traffic at all. So Ross had lied about why he had to leave the restaurant. She wondered what he knew about the caves and the beating that Jim and the other man took. When Jim had walked into the restaurant, Ross didn't bat an eye. What did it all mean? Both Jim and Ross had warned her away from moving into the lighthouse. But they were obviously on opposite sides of whatever was going on down there. Maybe she'd soon have a chance to talk to Jim and get his version of what was happening. Before she got into any kind of relationship with him, she had to know the truth. And with the way her heart was leading her to Jim, she knew that a relationship was inevitable. She couldn't deny its pull.

Mikela's eyes swept back and forth over both sides of the two-lane causeway. There was no sign of debris, no burnt-out flares, nothing to indicate any sort of accident had happened within the past couple of hours. What little she could see of the inky black water showed only mildly choppy waves. The breeze had picked up before she'd left the island and the moon was playing hide-and-seek behind the clouds rolling overhead, so she hoped that finding the driveway to Jim's house wouldn't be too difficult. When she saw the mainland up ahead, she knew that she was within fifteen or twenty minutes of Jim's home and needed to keep alert for the hidden drive. The road was tree-lined and fairly flat without any distinguishing landmarks to point the way or help her remember her only visit. White birch, sugar maples and oaks. Where were all the pine trees she remembered from the storm?

She was grateful for the earliness of the hour. At least there wasn't much traffic to slow her down or block her view of the drive. She hadn't seen any lights in her rearview mirror and there hadn't been any approaching traffic. She was certain she'd made it to the mainland without being followed. She kept watch for mailboxes, but there were none to be seen. As the road made a curve to the right, she saw the shattered remains of the oak tree that had almost toppled on her vehicle the other day. Neatly next to it was a pile of logs that had been cut from the body of the oak, obviously left there by the road-cleaning crew after the storm. She had driven too far. Mikela slowly turned around and retraced her path.

"Abby, where's your house?" Abby sat up in the front seat once again as Mikela kept her speed at 30 miles an hour. She turned the high beams on to get a better look at the side of the road. She'd gone another mile or so when Abby gave a little whine in her throat, just as Mikela saw a break in the wall of trees. She turned to the right and went over the now familiar potholes and dips, following the dirt path until it dead-ended at the two majestic oaks with the wooden steps. Abby danced in the passenger seat, eager to be home.

"Jim, we're home. Jim!" Niska sat up and began licking his master's face. "Hang on, Niska, I'll let you out the back."

Mikela shut off her engine and got out of the vehicle, with Abby right behind her. She walked to the rear of the SUV and opened the back. She'd put both men in from the passenger seats and had lain them back with their heads by the back door so all she'd have to do to pull them out would be to hook her hands under their arms and drag them backward.

"Jim, I need to get your front door open. Where's the key?" The only sound from Jim was another muffled moan. Mikela tried each pocket on his jacket, inside and out, and the pocket of his flannel shirt. No keys. She slid her hand inside his jeans pocket and found a small ring of keys. She pulled her hand out and held the keys up to the moon to see them better. Two keys appeared to be Ford keys, probably to his truck. Three more keys were on the chain. She smiled.

"I've got them, Jim! Just hang on, sweetheart. We're almost there."

She went to the front door and felt with her fingers until she found the deadbolt lock and slid in one of the keys. She heard the click of the bolt and pushed hard on the front door until it swung slowly inside. Mikela found a light switch and light flooded the living room. She walked quickly to the bedroom and opened the door wide. She would bring Jim inside first. She then went back to the living room and pushed the pillows from the couch. She would put the other man here. She quickly marched into the kitchen to locate the telephone and had to feel her way along the wall to turn on the lights. She would search for Jim's sister's phone number when she had them all safely inside the house.

Mikela walked through the living room to the front door. As she made her way down the steps, a bright light lit the entire front of Jim's house. She saw the dogs backlit by the brightness and put her hands up to her face. "What's going on? Jim!" she screamed as she heard the clicks of a dozen gun bolts being drawn.

"F.B.I. Drop your weapon. Put your hands behind your head," came a booming voice from out of the glare of the white light. Mikela froze in her tracks as rough hands came out of the darkness, bound her arms painfully behind her back and dragged her away from the house.

Chapter Fourteen

Mikela rubbed her skin where the plastic restraints used to bind her wrists had cut off her circulation. She had stood by in silence in the frenzy of activity that followed her capture by the F.B.I. A helicopter had landed in the space between Jim's back door and the outside workshop of his home, a fully-trained medical team on board. After being released, she watched as Jim's vital signs were taken, IVs inserted and he was hooked up to equipment that looked like the command center from a NASA launch. She couldn't be certain, but from the lack of equipment used on the other man, Mikela thought he might have died enroute from Beam Island. Hurting, depressed and alone, she was, once again, running on raw nerves—another sleepless night, an assault from Ross and now this. No one would let her close enough to Jim to tell him goodbye. She was emotionally and physically drained and without being able to see Jim, she felt her heart leave her body to go with the helicopter, destination unknown. She was nothing but an empty shell. She wandered over to the front steps of Jim's home and sat down, elbows on knees, her head in her hands. She couldn't even muster the energy to cry. She tried to sort out all the details of what happened the last couple of days but she couldn't keep her thoughts in any sort of order. She let out a deep sigh. She felt the nearness of one of the dogs and looked up to see Abby.

"Hey, girl. Your dad's going to be alright." Niska came trotting up the steps and turned around, he sat shoulder to shoulder with Mikela. She leaned back and opened her arms wide, hugging a dog under each arm.

"You two are the greatest," Mikela whispered. Abby licked Mikela's ear.

A shadow fell between Mikela and the lights of the official vehicles. "So, Mikela Williams. You've had quite an adventure over the past couple of days, eh?" Mikela looked up at the owner of the gravelly female voice. She was surprised to see an attractive woman about her own age staring down at her. She had long, black hair and brown eyes, athletic build, dressed in a black pantsuit, and held onto a little notepad. Despite the husky voice, the woman was very feminine as Mikela noticed the lace peeking from her suit jacket and the long, slender, painted fingernails.

"Yes, I guess so," Mikela sighed.

"I'm Special Agent Strongheart. Angela to my friends." One of the beautifully manicured hands reached out to Mikela, who relinquished her hold on Abby and Niska and took Angela's hand in a firm grip.

"Jim's sister?" asked Mikela, noticing how alike they were in coloring and facial features, especially around the eyes.

"Yes," said Angela. "I'm sorry about all the mystery surrounding Jim. By now I guess you've figured out that he's pretty important to us. In more ways than one," she smiled. Angela gave each of the dogs a pat and sat down to join the trio on the top step. "I don't know how much he's told you about what he does, but I think I'd better fill you in."

"Angela, do you mind if we go inside and do this over coffee? My mind isn't working at full speed right now."

"I'd love some. Agents Wilson and Davis will be in shortly and I'm sure they could use some, too." The women and dogs walked into the house and headed for the kitchen. Angela filled the coffee pot while Mikela took the can of coffee out of the refrigerator and together they pulled out mugs, milk, sugar and spoons and set everything down on the kitchen table. Mikela looked through the cupboards until she found the dog food and filled up the dogs' bowls with chow and water.

The coffee finished brewing as the two other agents entered the kitchen. Angela made the introductions and Mikela dutifully shook hands all around. She noticed that Abby and Niska had no objection to the men entering the room and guessed they must have already met. Everyone sat at the kitchen table, the three F.B.I. agents watching as Mikela doctored her coffee. She looked up and gave them a weary smile.

"Light and sweet," she offered, stirring until the liquid turned beige. "Old habits die hard." She took a sip and smiled. It was perfect. "Okay, I'm ready as I'll ever be to hear what this is all about."

Angela took the lead. "Well, Mikela, first of all, we're counting on your absolute discretion in this matter. It involves your inheritance of the lighthouse on Beam Island." She exchanged meaningful looks with her fellow agents. Agent Davis gave his head a slight nod in Angela's direction. "Despite your overseas connections, you've been granted a special security clearance and once you know the details, it's possible that you'll want to go to a safe house, at least until this is over. It's just incredibly bad timing that you happened to arrive this weekend, when we are mounting an all-out attack against Black Tide, the terrorist group."

Mikela's eyebrows shot up. She'd just read of another attack they'd made in Europe. Always at an airport, seemingly the flight preceding or following one of Mikela's courier trips. Truth be told, Black Tide was the deciding factor in Mikela's decision to quit her corporate courier job with WorldTron and move to the lighthouse. She carried the fear with her that any flight she took might be her last.

"I see you've heard of them. Of course, in your line of work, you would have," said Angela. "I'm afraid we hadn't yet cleared you through secure channels when you and Jim first met or he would have explained all this to you himself. You see, Black Tide has a smuggling branch that filters contraband from Europe to the U.S. and on through Canadian provinces. Your lighthouse is literally their beacon to the world. Their covert operations center is headquartered beneath your inheritance, in the maze of underground caves that run directly below you. That's why Jim acted like he did when you wouldn't stay here for a few days or turn around and go back home. He knew you would be in great danger."

"How do you know all this? That Jim tried to talk me into staying for a few days? I remember now that he was furious with me when I insisted on leaving." Had he really talked to his sister about her?

"Frankly, Mikela, you've been under surveillance for quite some time. You could have been a courier for Black Tide. We had to be absolutely certain you weren't one of their operatives." Agent Wilson said as he poured himself a second cup of coffee and topped off Angela's cup as well. "More for you?" he asked Mikela. She nodded her head and slid her cup in his direction.

"I just don't know what to make of all this," Mikela admitted. "I don't understand what the lighthouse has to do with it. It's been deserted for years. I just had the power and water turned on today—er, yesterday, actually. There are cobwebs everywhere. No one's been in there. I can understand how the caves would come in handy, but not what my house has to do with this." She began adding sugar and milk and stirring absent-mindedly.

"The caves are an underground network. The entrance is under the bluff side of the lighthouse and the underground tunnels are like a huge maze, some paths leading nowhere, others leading to remote areas on the mainland and even surfacing in Canada. Since it's difficult to access the inside, it's the perfect location for illegal operations. Some chambers are used for biological experimentation, others for manufacturing detonating devices. Still others are the holding areas for enemies of the United States as they are briefed on U.S. practices and customs before infiltrating their way into the country. Quite a few people that need to disappear for extended periods of time end up under the lighthouse. It's really very complex. If we can destroy the nerve center of their operation, the group itself would disband and agents would be ready at each exit of the maze, ready to take the terrorists into custody. We need the lighthouse. It's the best access to the maze."

Mikela looked thoughtfully into her cup of coffee. "And just how do you propose to do all that without being noticed?"

"Well, Mikela, we have several choices. Since you've made the acquaintance of some of the islanders already, you can help us by going back to the lighthouse, moving in as you had planned and carrying on 'business as usual'; or you can 'get the hell out of Dodge' while we plant a cover in your place; or we can set you up with a new identity in a new location and you can start your life all over again in another part of the country and forget all this ever happened and Uncle Sam will give you fair market value for the lighthouse. It's up to you."

"Doesn't seem like I have much of a choice. I want to keep the lighthouse. It's all I have left of my parents and I want to make it my home. I also need to be where Jim can find me when he gets out of the hospital." She looked up at Angela, trying to read her thoughts. Angela's face broke out in a smile.

"Jim told me you were one gutsy woman, Mikela! He told me a few other things, too, but I'll leave those comments for Jim to tell you himself when he recovers." Angela patted Mikela's forearm in a conspiratorial gesture. "For now, here's the plan…we didn't uncover any gun permits or evidence of a firearm sold to you since your eighteenth birthday. Is that right, you're unarmed?" Mikela nodded her head. "Okay," Angela continued. "You'll be furnished with a weapon and you'll learn how to use it." Mikela's eyebrows shot up in surprise. "We don't want you putting a bullet in your own foot in case of an emergency," Angela laughed. "You'll be briefed on the operatives who will be working with you and we'd like them to have access to the lighthouse, possibly as roommates. We'll work on that scenario. I wish we could tell you how long this will take, but I'm afraid at this point, we really don't know. We're hoping it will wrap up quickly and you can get on with your life."

Mikela took another long sip of coffee, put her cup down and swallowed. It didn't take her long decide what to do. "Okay. When do I start?"

Agent Davis reached over and shook her hand again. "Thanks, Mikela. The first thing we need to do is get our equipment inside the lighthouse and functioning. We'll need access to the beacon and the top floor. Any problem with that?"

"The truth is that I haven't even been to the top yet. Not in the last ten years, anyway. I had a visitor who snooped around while I was in the bathroom yesterday evening. He was headed upstairs when I went into the bathroom and when I came out, he'd disappeared. Turns out he was in the bedroom and had discovered a shaft that led down under the lighthouse. He said it only went down fifteen or twenty feet and tapered down to where a body wouldn't fit. He thought it was a storm shelter of some sort or a place for smugglers to hide. He may be one of Black Tide's operatives, I'm not sure. It seems like he was intent on snooping around, then he took me out to eat and in the middle of dinner, when I discovered Jim was hurt, he took off, making up a lie about an accident on the causeway. There was no accident on the causeway that I could see." Mikela looked up at the eyes intently focused on her.

"Ross Daniels," said Agent Wilson. "He's two-bit bagman for Black Tide. He doesn't even know who he's moonlighting for. We were just about to wing him yesterday when you let the big dog out of your SUV. In fact, I may just wing him for the hell of it. He's nothing but a punk. You're not the first woman he's attacked. He was transferred from another state police barracks in southern Maine. Apparently he thinks he's quite the ladies' man, but when his wife confronted him and let him know that she was divorcing his ass, he beat the tar out of her. His commander 'slapped his wrist' by making him take anger management classes and transferring him as far from his ex-wife as possible. I hate anyone who beats up on women or kids." Wilson's face was twisted in a grimace and he bent his spoon as he spoke. He looked at Angela and pursed his lips. "Go on, tell her Angela. We've told her everything else."

Angela colored a bit as she paused a moment to tell her story. "Well, Mikela, I've always known that I could take care of myself. But with this Ross character, he hit me so fast that I never knew what was coming. My cover was blown with Black Tide about six months ago. Somehow, Daniels found out I was F.B.I. He had his hands around my throat before I could react and crushed my neck. It was several weeks before I could speak and I'll never be able to sing again. He left me for dead, Mikela. Thank God Wilson was coming for me that night, or I would never have made it." Angela patted Wilson's thigh and Mikela noticed the look that passed between them.

"Well, since you know about my run-in with Ross, I guess I don't have to worry about who to tell. I wasn't sure who to report a state trooper to, but I knew it had to be done. He didn't seem to think that I'd

stay angry with him for trying to rape me." Mikela sadly shook her head.
"The man's worse than a two-bit thug or even a traitor. He's a psycho."
Mikela shivered at the memory. "Are you sure you want me to have a
loaded gun? Seems to me he'd make a good target for practice."

Chapter Fifteen

"Okay, Sophie. Thanks. I just didn't want to you worry about me disappearing for a couple of days. As soon as I get back from Bangor and have the furniture set up, I'll give you a call. You're sure you don't mind letting Joe Donnelly know I won't be back for a few days? Thanks so much, Sophie. Give my love to Otis. Okay. I'll drive carefully, I promise. Thanks…Bye!" Mikela looked across the table at Angela as she hung up the phone. "Well, that's done. That leaves Ross as the only person that might be wondering where I'm at, but he said he'd be back in a couple of days, so there's probably nothing to worry about with him—yet."

Angela's hand automatically went to her throat at the mention of Ross' name. The two women had spent the last few hours planning their strategy and keeping in touch with the medical team that had air-lifted Jim to the hospital in Bangor. Jim was expected to make a slow recovery. His partner, Matt Reynolds, wasn't so lucky. He was in a coma and fighting for his life with broken ribs and a ruptured spleen in addition to other internal injuries. His prognosis was grim. Jim had been able to speak briefly with Angela, telling her that Matt had been beaten with a piece of pipe.

"Thank God you showed up when you did, Mikela, or my brother would be dead by now." Angela said with tears in her eyes. "You have no idea how cruel these Black Tide people can be. Jim and Matt were lucky to have only been beaten. I'm so grateful to you." She squeezed Mikela's hand for emphasis and then let go, the emotional moment over. She cleared her throat and tried to get back her professional stance. "We'll stop in and see him when we get to Bangor. Why don't we pick out your furniture first and give him a few more hours to sleep? We'll have some lunch and maybe he'll be rested up enough to thank you himself." Angela gave Mikela another conspiratorial grin. The two women had immediately taken a liking to each other. Mikela wondered if this was what it was like to have a sister. Beneath the grim task that lay before them, there was a *comraderie* between them that the seriousness of the situation couldn't take away. No matter what the future held for her and Jim, she felt Angela would always be her friend.

"I'm ready when you are, Angela." Mikela rinsed the coffee cups in the kitchen sink before locking up the house and joining Angela, Davis and Wilson in the little non-descript car that was already running. As they headed down the highway for Bangor, the group discussed their plan to make sure nothing had been left to chance; Wilson taking notes as changes occurred. After outfitting Mikela with a weapon and spending some time on the firing range, the women would be dropped off to shop in Bangor, choosing furniture needed for the lighthouse. When they were ready, Angela would make a call and the furniture would be loaded into a special van with two F.B.I. agents doing double-duty as delivery men. The same afternoon of the furniture delivery, Mikela's 'cousins', Wilson and Davis, would stop by to visit on their yearly fishing trip. They would have a boat waiting for them in the marina for off-shore surveillance while Angela, in disguise, would stay at the lighthouse with Mikela. Satellite and radio equipment would be installed in the tower of the lighthouse. They would have state-of-the-art surveillance cameras and eavesdropping equipment. Mikela was fascinated, listening to the agents talk 'shop' and seeing how the plan to stem the horror of Black Tide unfolded. Despite her interest in their conversation, Mikela's foremost thoughts were of Jim and being able to see him this afternoon. Her heart leapt as she remembered their last kiss at the entrance of the cave.

The afternoon was a whirlwind of training and shopping. Mikela quickly learned how to break down, clean and shoot her weapon. Shopping was another chore she didn't relish, but with Angela's assistance, she actually enjoyed it. She chose a Danish sleighbed style for her bedroom suite and comfy, overstuffed country pieces for the main room. She purchased three large bookcases to hold her collection of antique books and murder mysteries, still in storage in New York. In the back of her mind, she was shopping for furnishings that not only pleased her, but would please Jim as well. She wanted her 'castle' to be a safe, comforting haven for both of them. Mikela was almost embarrassed as she realized how far her day-dreams had wandered from the reality of their situation. Although they each had rescued the other, there had never been any words of love be-tween them. She was acting like a school girl and would have to take things slow. Jim would be a long time in mending and she would need to get her life organized as soon as this adventure was over. Her thinking, now back on a more realistic track, made her realize she needed to shop for more mundane things—clothes, an ironing board and iron! She needed groceries, too, but she could get most of her supplies from McHenry's and get in a visit with Sophie and Otis, too.

Angela must have read her thoughts, because after seeing the new furniture safely loaded into the van, she whispered something to Wilson and waved the men away. She then hailed a cab and as they slid into the back seat, Angela told the driver, "Take us to the mall!"

Mikela bought a couple pair of jeans, some casual tops and another baggy sweatshirt. She would worry about dressier clothing later. She just wanted to look nice when she saw Jim in a couple of hours.

They stopped at a salon in one of the mall's department stores. Mikela had her hair washed, while Angela shopped for a wig. Mikela leafed through the latest *People* magazine as Angela had her beautiful nails cut short. Angela disappeared around a corner after having her nails done as Mikela walked up to the receptionist to pay for her pampering.

A rather brassy woman in an awful animal print outfit came up to the counter and stood next to Mikela, trying on different hairclips and posing in front of the mirror on the counter. "Honey, is this my color?" she de-manded. Mikela turned and mumbled something incoherent to the woman.

"Now, darlin', you didn't *really look*, did ya?" Annoyed, Mikela turned to face the woman and saw the twinkle of Angela's eyes.

"Oh, my gosh! That's great! I'd never have known it was you, Angela!" she laughed. Giving Angela the once-over, she whispered, "But walk behind me, will you? I don't want anyone to think we're together!" Together, they laughed their way out to the parking lot and signaled for a cab.

Back at the firing range, where Mikela went through the entire process of breaking down, cleaning and loading her weapon once more, she felt confident that she'd be able to defend herself without getting shot in the foot. While Angela chatted with the instructor, Mikela ducked into the ladies' room and changed into a new pair of jeans and a pretty new top in her favorite shade of 'seafoam' green. She washed her face and added a touch of color to her lips and cheeks. She took a deep breath, as the anticipation of seeing Jim made her heart beat faster. She walked up to Angela and the range instructor who was flirting with her. Obviously, the man was quite captivated by the woman in the leopard print blouse.

Chapter Sixteen

Mikela peeked around the corner from the empty hallway into the hospital room, watching as a nurse checked the flow of the IV drip attached by thin, clear tubing to a needle in Jim's arm. The nurse fiddled with a little button attached to the tube, pausing to make some notations on her clipboard. She spoke to her patient, but Mikela couldn't make out the words. A small television suspended from the ceiling kept up a constant stream of chatter, something about world events. The nurse stepped aside and patted her patient's arm. "I'll be back in a little while. Get some rest, Agent Strongheart." The nurse turned and smiled at Mikela, stopped to scan the barcode on the identification tag that Mikela had clipped to her shirt. "Well, Miss Williams, I believe someone's been hoping to see you." The nurse left the room and continued on down the hall as Mikela stood listening for the series of beeps that let her know the door locks had been secured after the nurse, also an F.B.I. agent, passed through to the unsecured part of the hospital.

Mikela walked slowly to the side of Jim's hospital bed. "Hello, Jim," she spoke softly. Laying her purse on a nearby chair, she leaned her hip against the side of his bed railing and ran her fingers over the skin of his wrist. His eyelids flickered and he smiled weakly as he recognized the face in front of him.

"Mikela," he whispered. "Are you okay?" He turned his hand over so her fingers slid into his palm and gave her a light squeeze. "You must be my guardian angel. You saved my life."

Mikela smiled. "I guess we're even, then." Jim patted the bed with his hand and Mikela sat down, careful of leaning too heavily against him. "I don't know if your nurse would like this," she teased.

"I won't break," he said, "I'm just sore as hell. I hurt in places I didn't even know I had. But I made out a lot better than Matt. Have they told you how he's doing?" Mikela looked deeply into Jim's eyes, not knowing what to say. She held his hand tighter.

"I know he has internal injuries, Jim. It doesn't look too good, but he's still hanging in there. He—he's in a coma right now." Mikela felt the tears well up in her eyes. She had wanted to keep cheerful in front of Jim, but the thought of how close he had been to death, made him all the more precious to her.

"Come here, Mikela." Jim reached up and held onto Mikela's arms, pulling her down to his level. She gently touched his lips with her own, being very careful not to add any pain to the burden he was already dealing with. "Will you stay at my house until I get out of here? You'll be safe and I won't have to worry about Niska and Abby getting lonely." He tried to hold her close but Mikela could see the pain in his eyes and gently wriggled free of his embrace.

"Don't worry, Jim. I'll take good care of them for you. Or maybe I should say they're taking good care of me. Please don't worry about anything. Just get better. And don't think for one minute I'm not waiting for you to keep your promise." Mikela leaned down and kissed him gently. "You've still got a lot of explaining to do." Jim drifted off to sleep with a crooked smile on his lips. Mikela kissed his forehead and patted his arm, hoping to see his eyes open again, but realizing that he would probably be out for hours.

She picked up her purse from the seat of the chair and stood for a moment, lost in thought about what lie ahead of her for the next several days, weeks, or months…she didn't know which. What she did know for certain was that Black Tide had to be destroyed and she would gladly do her part to see that it was done. She gave Jim a farewell kiss and took a long look, etching the memory of his bruised face in her mind.

With a resolve born partly of anger and partly of fear, she reluctantly left Jim's side and walked down the corridor to the heavy steel doors that kept the world at bay. As her identification tag scanned and was approved, the heavy doors slid silently open and then whooshed closed. The series of beeps were muted as the closing doors broke the dim murmur made by the agents awaiting Mikela's arrival in the unsecured section of hallway. As she joined them, Davis, Wilson and Angela stopped talking and looked at their new civilian teammate. "Let's do it." With determination in her stride, Mikela led the foursome out of the hospital and into the waiting cab.

Chapter Seventeen

The convoy crossed over the causeway and made its way onto the island, passing under the "Welcome to Beam Island" sign that had excited Mikela just a few days earlier. She drove her SUV through the main street of the downtown area, passing by McHenry's, the little post office and library. She didn't notice Ross' patrol car or his Corvette, but kept on the alert for both. Several miles later, she passed beneath the canopy of trees that opened onto the sand and gravel driveway leading to the historic lighthouse that harbored dark secrets, both old and new, far below its beacon tower. Mikela arrived first and then the delivery truck pulled up to the front door. The third vehicle, a utility truck with the logo of a satellite dish company pulled alongside the delivery truck. As Mikela and Angela exited the vehicle, the dogs bounded out past them. Niska and Abby excitedly sniffed the ground around the lighthouse door where they'd thwarted Ross Daniels' plans. Mikela and Angela entered the lighthouse as Wilson and Davis began to unload the truck. Davis looked around and scouted out the area of trees as well as the bluff side of the lighthouse, while Wilson unfastened the dolly and leaned it against the outside of the truck, although he doubted they'd be using it.

On the drive to Beam Island, Angela had briefed Mikela on a few things that she'd need to remember over the next couple of weeks. They had picked the name "Hazel" as Angela's undercover name while she was posing as Mikela's cousin from New York.

When first entering the lighthouse, the agent in the satellite truck would scan every inch, top to bottom, to locate any bugging devices, audio or video. The radio and satellite equipment would be installed in the beacon tower area. Four agents would arrive in the satellite truck but only two would be seen to enter and only two would actually leave. There would be an agent stationed in the beacon tower 24/7 to cover any transmissions coming to or from the caves via satellite or short wave, leaving the other free to do night reconnaissance around the entrance to the underground tunnels. Within a matter of a few short hours, Black Tide's secret transmissions would be beamed to F.B.I. agents the world over.

Mikela was high on an adrenaline rush, excitement in every step. She was happy to be furnishing her new home and proud to be a part of the mission to disband Black Tide. She felt safe with Angela and the other agents and well-protected with Abby and Niska at her side. Jim was going to recover and they'd have a chance at a life together. She hummed and smiled as she oversaw the placement of the bedroom furniture.

"Hazel, I'm getting hungry. How about you? We need to get some groceries—I haven't had a chance to do any real shopping yet." Mikela had just finished putting fresh sheets on her new mattress when Angela signaled they should go into town. She spoke loud enough so that if there were any listening devices, the eavesdroppers might want to pay a quick visit while they were out running errands.

"Honey, I'm famished," said 'Hazel', in her New York voice. "What do you feel like? I could eat a horse right about now. You wanna get take-out or are we cooking here?" If Mikela hadn't seen the transformation for herself, she'd have never believed it was Angela underneath the red hair and outlandish clothes. It was hard not to laugh at her antics and Mikela had to be extra careful. The only secure area where they could talk was in her vehicle that had been checked stem-to-stern at the F.B.I.'s transport building. She had a little button on her key ring that would flash a red light if any detection devices not of the F.B.I.'s making were found on the vehicle in the future. "Youse don't' have to tell me twice, either, honey. I'm ready!" The two women grabbed their purses and let the delivery men know they'd be going out.

"We'll be back in an hour or so," Mikela told Wilson and Davis. "Can we bring you a sandwich or something back from town?" Angela took Wilson aside into the kitchen and gave him a quick kiss goodbye, assuring him in hushed whispers that they wouldn't be long. She'd be scoping out the older couple Mikela would be introducing her to, who ran the island's store. She'd also try and get a fix on Ross Daniels. She sashayed out of the kitchen and back into the main room.

Wilson and Davis had already unloaded the couch, overstuffed chairs, end tables and lamps into the middle of the big room, which would be the main living area of the lighthouse. While the two agents had been unloading the truck, the other four agents had managed to get inside the lighthouse and had their equipment and bugging checks in the lower level and had taken the rest of the equipment upstairs. Mikela had pointed out the hatch cover in the secret room behind the bedroom closet. She was eager to see if the agents would discover that Black Tide had already made some sort of use of her parents' summer home. She wanted to hurry into town so they could get back and see if anything had been uncovered in their absence.

The women left the house together and got into Mikela's SUV, with the dogs sitting in the back seat. On the drive into town, Mikela speculated on what would happen if they ran into Ross. As it turned out, they wouldn't have to wait very long to find out. She pulled into a parking space in front of McHenry's—across from the state trooper's patrol car parked across the street. She watched as Angela put her hand to her throat. "It'll be okay, Angela. You look so different. He'll never know it's you. And we'll leave the dogs right outside the door. Please don't worry." Mikela patted her friend's arm.

"I should be reassuring you, not the other way around. I know it'll be alright…I just re-live that moment every time I think of him," Angela shuddered as she spoke. "Ok, I'm alright. Let's get the introductions over with. And don't forget my name's Hazel!" Angela gave Mikela a 'thumb's up' sign and a big smile as she climbed out of the passenger side of the vehicle. The 'thumb's up' was returned as Mikela exited out of the driver's side, the dogs following on her heels. Together they all went up the wooden steps to the door. Mikela gave the command to sit before entering the store and Niska and Abby dutifully sat on their haunches.

Sophie was at the cash register as the women walked in. "Mikela! How did everything go in the big city? Are you all moved in, dear?" She rushed around the counter and gave Mikela a welcoming hug. "And who's your friend?" she said, touching Angela's arm.

"Sophie, this is my cousin Hazel from New York. She's going to stay with me until I get all settled in." 'Hazel' and Sophie shook hands as Mikela made the introductions. "She's an ace decorator and I need all the help I can get," she laughed. "Sophie's the lady that makes the best coffee in the universe and her pastries are out of this world." Sophie blushed with pride and shrugged off the compliment.

"You'd better let the boys know you're here, dear. Otis' been wondering how you're doing and Ross is with him, crying about you being out of town."

"Ross hasn't said anything to you about the other night?" Mikela was astounded.

Sophie's eyebrows shot up in a quizzical expression. "No, he didn't. Only that he got called away early from your date—do we need some 'girl talk' here?"

At that moment Ross walked up to the trio of ladies. "Well, well, well…what's all this whispering about? Hello, sweetheart. Who's your friend?" Ross took Mikela's hands in his and gave her a peck on the cheek. Mikela visibly stiffened at his touch and pulled her hands away.

"Th-this is my cousin—Hazel. She's staying with me for a while."

"Hazel. Nice to meet you." Ross shook hands with her, and covered her hand with both of his, holding on longer than was necessary. "I'm sure I'll be seeing a lot of you. Mikela and I are old friends already. Better than friends, actually." Angela felt his steely gray eyes going right through her. It was all she could do not to cover her throat with her hand, but she managed to maintain her composure as Ross' eyes wandered slowly from her face down the length of her body and back up to her eyes. "Be seein' you, ladies." Ross donned his trooper hat and touched the rim, his trademark gesture. Sophie noticed that both women were relieved when he left the store.

"Sophie, he acted like a psycho. You were here when I met him—I barely know him at all. He showed up to take me to dinner the night Joe Donnelly came to turn on the water…" Mikela's story was interrupted by the deep growling of a male dog.

"What's that noise?!" Sophie looked alarmed. She looked from Mikela to Hazel and back again.

"Come on outside for a second, Sophie, I want you to meet some more of my friends." Mikela headed toward the front door. They watched from behind the screen as Ross Daniels bolted down the front steps and into his car, slamming the door. He quickly backed his car out of the parking space and squealed his tires as he rushed off. Mikela pushed the door open and held it for Sophie and Hazel. "Niska. Abby. Meet Sophie." Both dogs raised their left paws in unison. Sophie laughed delightedly, shaking each dog's paw.

"Well, they're just beautiful!" Sophie exclaimed, ruffling both of the animals' soft wool. "Otis, come on out here!" Otis was already on his way toward the front of the store. Mikela introduced Otis to Hazel, Niska and Abby. The dogs politely shook hands with the older man. A young mother and her two children stopped to pet the dogs. Otis handled the introductions while Sophie herded Mikela and Hazel back into the store. "Now tell me the rest of the story."

"Well, he showed up at the lighthouse saying I'd made a date for dinner with him. And I might have. It was the day I came in and fell asleep in the back room. I was so tired that I really don't remember much of anything. But I got home and told Joe what I wanted done and went for a walk. I came back and Ross was there. We went to The Fish Tale for dinner—"

"He took you *there*?" Sophie exclaimed in surprise, shaking her head. "That place has the reputation of being a really rough joint!"

"We didn't stay for long. We'd just started eating and I got up to use the restroom and when I came back he was ready to go. Said he'd gotten a call and had to work an accident on the causeway and had to bring me home right away. So he took me back home and I got in my SUV and went to look for the dogs. I wasn't gone 15 minutes. When I got back, he was in my driveway and accused me of cheating on him!" Mikela huffed as Sophie continued to shake her head in disbelief. "I told him I barely knew him and the next thing I knew, he was all over me! If it wasn't for the dogs, I would've been raped. Then he told me he'd see me in a couple of days, like nothing had ever happened. So that's when I decided I needed to put some distance between us and went into Bangor and picked out my furniture. Then I met Hazel at the airport and here we are. I think I'll be a lot safer if she stays with me until he gets a grip." Sophie nodded in agreement.

"I don't know what to say. He seems so mannerly, but you just never know about a fellow. What do you think of him, Hazel?" The women stopped talking as Otis came in with the kids and their mom. "Well, I'd best get back to work. What can I help you with today?" Pulling Mikela to the side, she whispered, "We'll talk more later, dear."

"Did you make anything special for dinner tonight?" Mikela asked as she worked her way toward the tables near the kitchen. "Something smells wonderful." She led Hazel to the coffee counter and they filled up their cups with the steaming brew.

"Let's see. I've got lasagna, but you've already had that. Have you eaten at the Beachfront yet? Tonight's their seafood night. And I won't get mad if you eat there...that's my sister's place," Sophie laughed. Mikela and Angela gathered up plenty of breakfast items, breads and butter, along with a dozen of Sophie's homemade pastries, and a pan of frozen lasagna. Sophie had salads in take-out containers in the cooler and the girls took several of those, too. Sophie had Otis load a huge bag of dog food into Mikela's truck. "Looks like you two haven't eaten in a week," Sophie smiled as she bagged their purchases. After agreeing to meet back at the store in a day or two to finish their 'girl talk', Sophie hugged them both goodbye and walked them out. The two dogs jumped into the SUV as Mikela opened her door and Sophie poked her head in and handed a rawhide bone to each canine for a treat. "You two be careful now!" Sophie and Otis waved goodbye and walked back inside as another group of shoppers made their way up the wooden steps to McHenry's.

Chapter Eighteen

As Mikela, Angela and the dogs bumped up the driveway to the lighthouse in the SUV, they passed the satellite truck as it was heading back to the mainland. The two vehicles slowed and stopped next to each other. Mikela leaned back in her seat, so Angela could talk to the two men.

"You're all set, Agent Strongheart. We'll be back in a couple of days to relieve Hennessey and Johnson." Mikela was trying to count the freckles on the red headed agent's face as he spoke to Angela, updating her on their progress. In the shadows of the van, she couldn't tell which of the other agents was going back to the mainland for the next few days and which two were remaining behind.

"Thanks, Rick. We appreciate your hard work out here. Let's hope we can all go home soon." Angela waved to the men in the truck and sat back in her seat. "This is it, Mikela. Are you sure you don't want to follow them back? No one would think any less of you if you did."

Mikela turned to look Angela in the eye. "There's no way I'm leaving any of you behind. I can't imagine anything worse happening to me that hasn't already happened. Besides, I promised your brother I'd be waiting for him," Mikela grinned and playfully elbowed Angela in the side. Angela smiled back.

"I'm glad you're staying with us, but Jim's already going to kill me for not leaving you at his house...if anything happens to you, I hate to even think about what my brother would do to me!" They pulled up to the house. The moving van was still parked out front. As the women got out of the SUV, Niska and Abby jumped out of the vehicle and trotted into the lighthouse with their rawhide bones. Wilson and Davis came up the steps to help unload the groceries.

"This looks so terrific!" Mikela gushed as she walked down the steps into the cozy living area. "It feels like home already!" Niska had claimed a seat on the oversize couch and Abby was turning in circles on an overstuffed chair before finally settling in to chew her bone.

In the kitchen, Wilson and Davis helped Mikela and Angela get dinner ready. They decided on one of Sophie's frozen lasagnas and put one in the oven. The four would take dinner upstairs so Hennessey and Johnson could eat with them without leaving their post. Mikela was eager to see the upstairs, having not made a trip to the top of the beacon tower since her recent return to the island. Agent Wilson showed off his culinary skills by making a loaf of bread, no doubt hoping to impress Angela. Mikela smiled at all the looks and laughs that passed between the two agents and tried to keep her spirits up. The playful flirting between Angela and Wilson made her ache all the more for Jim, but she kept her feelings to herself. For the moment, every one let their guard down. The *comraderie* and good feelings in the air made the lighthouse a warm and inviting home. The only thing missing was Jim.

"A toast to Mikela. May she live a long and happy life, perched in her lighthouse!" Six paper cups met in the air over the center of the table, followed by laughter. Mikela blushed, murmured a 'thank you' and took a sip of her Coke.

"I'm full. I think I'll get some fresh air. You all need to finish this lasagna or you'll hurt Sophie's feelings." She got up from the table, crumpling her paper plate and napkin into the trash bag. She smiled around at her new friends, wondering how long it would be before Jim would be joining them for a dinner like this. She climbed the few steps in the center of the room and lifted the hatch, climbing out onto the widow's walk that surrounded the tower. The view where she stood was breathtaking. She could see miles and miles of ocean on the bluff side of the tower. As she

walked the circumference she could identify the tops of some of the build-
ings in the downtown area, the spire from the little church and she could
even make out the causeway in the distance. It was a beautiful and inspir-
ing view looking out over the tree tops. Lazy terns glided and dove on the
afternoon air currents. The ocean's brine was pungent today and she
took a deep breath before turning around to take the wooden steps back
down into the tower.

The following week dragged by. Mikela and Angela went to the mainland twice to visit with Jim. Mikela's heart would beat wildly when she
first saw him and each visit bound their hearts closer together. The F.B.I.
agents listening in the lighthouse tower didn't intercept any messages from
Black Tide that indicated activity would take place soon. Mikela, after a
lifelong interest in law enforcement, got a firsthand look at the mind-numbing
grind of surveillance. Hennessey and Johnson were recalled after install-
ing a relay transmitter that would reach their ears on the mainland. Another day of waiting and Black Tide still hadn't made any important transmissions. Mikela passed the time by working on her new home, decorat-
ing it with an eye for ease and comfort. Two of the bookcases were set
along either side of the fireplace and filled with her collection of antique
books. The third bookcase was placed in the bedroom and filled with her
favorite authors. At night she enjoyed sitting on the huge sofa between the
dogs and watching the firelight play on the old bindings. As Mikela pined
for Jim, Angela did the same for Wilson.

Thursday evening arrived and with it, Ross Daniels. Mikela made it
obvious that she was not pleased that he had come to the lighthouse. She
didn't allow him room to pass when he tried to barge his way in. With one
hand on the doorknob and the other holding the doorjamb, Ross took the
opportunity to grab her as he had that awful night after their 'date.'

"Get your hands off me!" she screamed, pummeling his chest with her
fists. His laughter quickly died as he saw Niska, Abby and Angela running
toward him; Angela had drawn her gun. He released his hold on Mikela
and as she fell from his grasp and onto the stair landing, Niska stood
between them and waited for Ross to make another move. Niska's hair

stood up from his back forming a spiked ridge all the way to his tail. He bared his teeth and growled a warning to Ross.

"Call him off, Mikela. Now." Ross' eyes grew big in his head, locked on the one hundred and twenty pound dog that would strike on command.

"Get out of here. I don't want you on my property. You've attacked me twice now and I'm not going for thirds. Just leave me alone," Mikela stood up, took a step back from Ross and spoke with a trembling in her voice.

"Nice friend you've got there. I'd shoot him for ya, honey, but I think it'd be more fun watchin' the dogs use him as a chew toy," 'Hazel' quipped.

"Mikela. Call-him-off-now." Ross hadn't moved a muscle and neither had Niska.

"Sit, Niska." Niska sat, but did not move from his position between Mikela and Ross. "Ross, go away and leave me alone. If you come near me again, I'm going to report you. I probably should report you anyway. If there is a next time, I'm not going to call Niska off."

Mikela walked up to close the door, refusing to act frightened. "You're going to be sorry, bitch. Real sorry. And so is your friend." Ross turned on his heel and walked away to his car. Mikela slammed the door shut with all her might.

She shook all the way to the couch and sat down hard. Tears were flowing, whether from rage or fear, she couldn't be certain. She was furious that this man was allowed to wear a badge. Abby climbed up on the couch to sit next to her, laying her head on Mikela's shoulder. Angela joined them and Niska lay down at the women's feet. "I can't believe he keeps doing this. He's scaring me, Angela. Really scaring me," Mikela sobbed into Abby's fur.

"I'll take care of things, don't worry about it. Don't let him get to you, Mikela. Psychos like him don't deserve any tears. I'm going to report in and see what they want me to do." Angela got up and went into the kitchen. Mikela could hear the murmur of a one-sided conversation. She gave Abby a kiss on the nose and ruffled both dogs' fur as she got up from the couch and went into the bathroom to wash her face.

"Mikela, do you think you can stand Ross for another week? They want us to hold off a few more days before pulling him off the island. Black Tide's been quiet way too long. They think something may happen in the next week to ten days," Angela broke the news somberly to Mikela. Both women desperately wanted the man behind bars and stripped of any authority or weapons that he had. They worried that he wouldn't only try to hurt them, but possibly the dogs, too. Thursday and Friday they stayed in the lighthouse, going out only to walk the dogs together. Friday night was uneventful and they started feeling cooped up, needing a change of scenery.

By Friday morning, the women were angry. Ross was nothing less than a terrorist and to keep hidden in the lighthouse would let him know that he could intimidate them into submission. They'd had enough. They were angry at Black Tide and they were angry at Ross Daniels. The boredom of surveillance was taking its toll on their spirits. And they were getting hungry. The food they'd bought at McHenry's a week ago had just about run out. Mikela needed her coffee and she needed it light and sweet. There was just enough milk left for one cup in the morning.

"Ok, Angela. I've had it. I guess I wasn't cut out for this secret agent stuff. If we're not going to report Ross, then let's forget about him for now. I can't stand it in here anymore!"

Her demand came out more like a plea, but Angela was all in favor of it. The two women were going to spend the whole day out. First thing in the morning, they would head out to the mainland and visit with Jim and Wilson. Then they'd come back to the island and spend the afternoon browsing the various shops and galleries that Beam Island offered. Dinner would be at one of the seafood restaurants followed by a last stop at McHenry's to do another week's worth of shopping. Angela radioed the news of their plans for the following day to the F.B.I.'s mainland office. When the women finally fell asleep, it was the first night since the attack on Mikela that neither woman had nightmares about Ross Daniels.

Chapter Nineteen

Mikela woke early on Saturday morning filled with eager anticipation of seeing Jim. She showered quickly and put on one of her favorite tops and her 'skinny' jeans. She didn't usually wear perfume but today she spritzed on her favorite fragrance, hoping to smell as good as she looked. She smiled to herself and hummed as she finished her hair and makeup. Angela was still asleep on the couch so Mikela thought she'd enjoy a quiet cup of coffee alone with her thoughts before waking Angela up. She poked through the cabinets to see what she could rustle up for breakfast and found that she had all the ingredients she needed to make something special to start off the day. After popping a pan into the oven, she quickly did the dishes and made a pot of coffee. She fed and watered the dogs when they returned from their morning patrol of the grounds and finally sat down to a glorious view of the sun rising out of the eastern sky.

"Mmm...cinnamon rolls!" smiled a groggy Angela as she padded into the kitchen. She poured coffee into her mug and took a tentative sip. "Ah, perfect!" Angela sat down and watched as Mikela set the hot pan from the oven onto a trivet in between them on the kitchen table. Removing the oven mitt, Mikela sat back in her chair and savored the last half of her morning coffee. She gingerly picked up a hot roll and put one on each of their plates.

Angela leaned over the roll and inhaled deeply. "Oh, this is so great, I'm starving!" she smiled. The women ate their first rolls in contented silence. By their second roll, they were talking excitedly about visiting Jim. Wilson would meet them at the hospital and they would all have lunch in Jim's room. The dogs picked up on the excitement and danced around the women, eager to see their 'dad' and their house. They rooted out their rawhide bones from underneath the couch cushions and sat impatiently at the door.

At long last, the SUV left the metal grating of the Beam Island bridge behind as all four tires touched down on the mainland's paved highway. Destination Bangor! Mikela and Angela both marveled at the beautiful day and the wondrous scenery. The world was looking brighter in their shared anticipation of the day to come. They stopped at Jim's house to water the plants and pick up a change of clothes for him, hoping for his quick release from the hospital. The dogs enjoyed exploring their yard again, back in familiar territory and ran for a romp in the woods. In less than half an hour, the group was back on the road, eager to be in the city. The wooded scenery changed to country homes, growing closer together as the countryside turned to city and they found themselves in the hospital parking lot. Hennessey and Johnson were there to greet them at the hospital's entrance and took Abby and Niska for a walk on the hospital lawn as the women entered the building. They passed through the secure area, where they were issued their bar coded identification tags. The women paused just a moment to clip the tags on their clothes and went on in through the metal doors and finally stood at the foot of Jim's bed.

"Hey, handsome!" Angela called out. Jim's bed was empty and the bathroom door was closed. The door slowly opened and Jim peeked around the corner, shaving cream covering the bottom half of his face. His face split in a happy grin and then a frown as he tasted the white foam. He turned back to the sink and rinsed the lather off his face. Angela and Mikela stood watching and laughing at the faces he made. He came out of the bathroom and grabbed a woman in each arm and they had a lingering group hug. He kissed Angela's cheek and then released her. Turning to Mikela, he held her by her shoulders and took a long look at the face he'd been missing for what seemed like an eternity. She reached her hands up to cup his chin, and forgetting that Angela was in the room with them, they hungrily shared a kiss.

"Oh, come on, you two! Get a room!" Angela joked. She sat down on the chair next to the hospital bed. Jim and Mikela finally pulled themselves apart, but continued to hold on, arms around each other's waists, neither wanting to break the physical connection.

"I've missed you, Mikela," Jim took her hand in his and kissed her fingers. "Are Niska and Abby taking good care of you?"

"Yes, they are. I just love them. I don't think I'll ever be able to give them back," Mikela looked deeply into Jim's dark eyes. She scanned his face and lifting herself up on her tiptoes, she kissed his lips and his cheek. "It's so good to hold you again. How are you feeling?"

"Great, now," Jim winked at Angela over Mikela's head. Angela smiled knowingly. Jim noticed that she perked up considerably as Wilson entered the room.

"Hey, can anyone join in?" he teased. Angela practically jumped out of the chair and sailed into Wilson's arms. They joined in a long awaited lip lock of their own. When they'd released each other, Wilson and Jim shook hands and decided it was time to update the women on the past week's events.

Wilson sat on the foot of the bed, looking grim. "As you all already know, Matt wasn't expected to make it out of his coma. And he didn't. He died this morning at 3a.m., another victim of Black Tide. His family's downstairs at the morgue now, awaiting release of his body to take back home. It's really awful. He has—had—a young wife and two kids. We'll pay our respects before we leave, if that's alright with everyone." He looked at each one in turn and they all nodded in silent agreement. Mikela held Jim's hand tighter, aware that it could have been him lying in the cold silence of the basement morgue. Tears welled in her eyes and as she leaned against him, he held her tighter, both of them painfully aware of the preciousness of life. Although the mood of the room was a sober one, each could feel the resolve beating in their hearts to do away with the menace of Black Tide.

"With this awful news, comes some good. Jim is going to be released today." At his announcement, Wilson smiled as he watched everyone's reactions to the good news. "And Jim and I are going to take a couple of gorgeous ladies out to lunch to celebrate." Mikela turned and kissed Jim so hard, he fell over backwards onto the bed. They laughed, embracing and kissing several times before standing up again. Angela gave her brother a hug and, smiling, dropped a paper bag into his hands, containing the change of clothes she'd picked up at his house for him earlier. As Jim changed into street clothing, Wilson filled Mikela and Angela in on the F.B.I.'s future plans for Black Tide's headquarters in the caves under Mikela's home. "Yesterday afternoon a Middle Eastern freighter anchored about ten miles northeast off the coast of Beam Island, presumably with engine trouble. The Coast Guard sent out a vessel to investigate, with F.B.I. agents posing as its crew. F.B.I. and Coast Guard intelligence reported that the foreign vessel was awaiting a delivery of some sort, probably land mines or biohazard weaponry that Black Tide was selling and the delivery's going down in the next 72 hours."

Jim walked out of the bathroom as Wilson finished relating the story of the freighter. "And what will we do now?" asked Mikela.

Jim's eyebrows shot up. "What do you mean, *we?* You're going to continue to stay at my place with Abby and Niska while the rest of us do our jobs! And then you and I are going to see about living 'happily ever after', Mikela Williams!" Jim had gathered his few personal items and placed them in the paper bag that Angela had given him. Jim's comment had caught Mikela off guard. She'd just assumed that someone had told him that she'd had the dogs at the lighthouse and was a sort of a temporary civilian agent.

"I like the sound of the 'living happily ever after' part, Jim, but hasn't anyone told you that I'm working with all of you on Black Tide?" Mikela innocently asked. "I just assumed that the first surveillance team had told you of the change in plans. We've been camped out at the lighthouse for over a week now."

Jim looked at Wilson and then Angela when he realized no one else was laughing with him. "Are you guys serious?" he demanded. "You can't be. There's no way I'm letting Mikela put herself in that kind of danger!" No one responded. Angela looked at her shoes as Wilson scanned the room.

Mikela sought out Jim's embrace as she tried to reason with him. She could feel him tense under her touch. "Here we go again with this macho thing. I love you for wanting to protect me, Jim, but no matter what, the lighthouse is my home and if the F.B.I. is going to use it to monitor Black Tide, then I'm in on it. I've already been issued a gun and have been trained on how to use it. Niska and Abby have been with me the entire time and at first, we had Hennessey and Johnson up in the beacon tower, with me and Angela downstairs. Nothing happened, so they pulled the guys out, but Angela, or should I say my 'cousin Hazel' has been with me the entire time. I'm perfectly safe." She looked up at him with her liquid eyes and his heart melted.

"I just can't believe you've been put in this kind of danger. Look at what happened to me and Matt. You know better than anyone what kind of shape you found us in, sweetheart. Do you think Black Tide will go easier on you because you're a woman? It would be worse. Women count for absolutely nothing to these men. Don't you understand why I can't let you be a part of this?" Jim pleaded with her. He was holding her by her shoulders, looking into her eyes as Wilson and Angela took the opportunity to quietly leave the room.

"Yes, Jim. I understand how you feel, and I don't want you to be angry with me, but I have to do my part. You don't seem to mind that Angela's a major player in all this and I know you care about what happens to her."

"Honey, Angela is a trained agent. You're not." He saw the look in her eye and continued. "Okay, okay. You're trained with a gun. But you haven't had to use it, have you?"

"Well, no, but that's because Niska and Abby were there and attacked him before I could get the gun out of my purse. But I was *going* to use it." As soon as Mikela realized what she'd said, she regretted it. "You were attacked?" he asked in disbelief. "By Black Tide agents?" She could see the concern on his face.

"No, a local jerk named Ross Daniels. He'd had too much to drink or something. I think he's some sort of psycho, but he won't bother me anymore. 'Hazel' and I ran into him grocery shopping last week and he left rubber on the pavement when he left the store, he was so scared of the dogs!" Mikela almost laughed at the memory. "He hasn't been around since then, so it's okay. Really." Mikela held Jim's hands in hers, trying to sound convincing. Jim looked as though he was going to lose his temper, but after a few moments and a few deep breaths, he seemed to calm down.

"Honey, I'm hungry for some real food and I want to talk this out. Maybe Angela and Wilson can help me convince you, although it looks like they wimped out on me already. I just can't believe an untrained civilian woman..." He sighed again and didn't bother finishing his sentence. What was he going to do with this woman? She definitely had a mind of her own.

"It's okay, Angela. You two can come back in," Jim hollered toward the doorway. He took the opportunity to kiss the petal soft lips of the beautiful woman that made him crazy and had saved his life. He held her close and savored her sweet smell, the velvety softness of her hair, the warmth of her nearness. Eyes closed, he smiled to himself, lost in the tender moment, realizing for the first time in a long time, what it felt like to fall in love.

The foursome walked through the doors of the secured hospital wing and into the main lobby, where they took another elevator that would bring them into the hospital's belly, the morgue. Matt's parents and wife huddled together in a grim little waiting area, eyes red-rimmed and swollen. Jim went to the group first, shaking hands and hugging. He was followed by Mikela, Angela, and Wilson who uttered their condolences, even though there were none to be had. Jim led the group in a quiet prayer and when it was finished, they left the grieving family with the promise that they would soon see the end of Black Tide, reassuring them that Matt had not died in vain. The somber group left the hospital together. They found Hennessey and Johnson with the dogs, sitting at a shaded picnic table on the hospital grounds. The dogs were literally 'jumping for joy' at the sight of Jim and he was just as happy to see them. Angela, Wilson and Mikela watchED the reunion in fascination. While Jim played with the dogs for a few moments, the agents briefed Angela and Mikela on news they'd intercepted from the Middle-East freighter. Angela needed to get into her role as 'Hazel' as soon as possible, and the two women would finish out their day as planned. After the four had lunch, the two women would return to Beam Island, be seen for an hour or two shopping around town, stop at McHenry's for a week's worth of groceries and then head back to the lighthouse, where they would meet up with Wilson and Jim. Angela had brought her 'Hazel' clothes and wig with her and would change quickly while they were at the hospital.

They all agreed on Chinese for lunch, Hennessey and Johnson begging off after agreeing they would meet up later that evening on Beam Island with the rest of the group. While Jim went back in with Wilson to sign some release forms, Mikela accompanied Angela to the ladies' room, to watch the transformation into Hazel. The ladies' room was for a single person so Mikela told Angela to meet her in the waiting area around the corner when she was ready. Leaving Angela safely locked inside to make her transformation , Mikela walked the few steps into the little waiting area of the hospital's emergency room. She browsed the magazine rack and smiled at an elderly gentleman that was sitting a few seats down from her. She opened up the latest issue of Newsweek to see what had been going on in the world since her last flight home to New York. It had been a long while since she'd read about world events, being so preoccupied with her own personal tragedy and the move to Beam Island.

After a few moments, Mikela looked up to see Hazel waving to her. She folded up her magazine and put it back into the rack. Hazel had a head start down the empty hallway and Mikela jogged to catch up with her. "Do you think you could put a little more wiggle into that walk, Hazel?" Mikela teased as she drew up alongside her. The mop of big red hair turned. It took a second to register that it wasn't Angela under the wig. With horror, Mikela turned to run away, but the elderly gentleman that had smiled at her just moments before now had her arms in a vise-like grip. Mikela struggled, trying to fight the handkerchief that was being held over her nose and mouth. The hallway spun around her as she weakened and finally disappeared into a black void.

Chapter Twenty

Mikela slowly became aware of the putrid stench of low tide as the throbbing in her head pounded her awake. She opened her eyes to an inky blackness, not knowing where she was. She tried to move her head, but the pain from the slight movement almost knocked her out again. She felt like she had a terrible hangover. Taking a few deep breaths to clear her head didn't help, either. The repulsive smell turned her stomach as she fought the urge to vomit. Once her stomach settled back down, the throbbing in her head began to ease and she started to remember following Angela down the hallway in the hospital. No, not Angela, someone wearing Angela's wig. The old man pinning her arms, something being held over her nose and mouth so she couldn't breathe. Her thoughts were interrupted by a low moan coming from the floor beside her in the dark. She rolled over and realized she was lying in some sort of wet muck. Getting to her hands and knees, she felt around in the dark in front of her, her hands patting what felt like damp stone until she touched an arm. She used her hands to try and identify who was next to her. Working her way up the arm, she felt a narrow shoulder, a slender neck and then a smooth face. No stubble or facial hair, so it was a woman's face under her fingers. She moved her hands to the top of the head and felt long, straight hair. "Angela? Angela is that you?" she whispered. No answer. "Angela, please wake up." The echoes of her whispers were spooky in the darkness. She gently shook the shoulder she hoped was Angela's, but it didn't do any good. Mikela sat still in the darkness, cross-legged on the cold stone floor, and tried to make sense of what was happening. If this woman next to her was Angela, then where were Jim, Wilson and the others? Had they been kidnapped, too, or were they still waiting at the hospital? She had no idea how long she'd been unconscious and she couldn't see her watch to tell what time it was. Surrounded by the damp darkness and odor of decay, she was certain that she was somewhere underneath the lighthouse in the maze of caves. She couldn't remember a thing after passing out, so it would do no good to try and find her way out of the caverns. She would have to wait it out.

A moan tore open the silence surrounding Mikela. It echoed off the walls and made Mikela's heart skip a beat. She turned and shook the shoulder of the body lying next to her. "Angela! Angela...It's okay...wake up. Please wake up!" she pleaded.

"Oh, my head! I can't see..." Angela's voice faltered as she tried to speak and gagged on the nauseating smell.

"Breathe through your mouth, Angela, it'll make the smell easier to take. Are you okay?" Mikela gently rubbed her friend's arm. "I'm so glad you woke up. I'm not sure where we are, but my guess is that we're somewhere underneath the lighthouse. Just lie still for a minute and see if you're alright. Your head's gonna hurt for a little while, but it'll go away."

"I can't believe this. What the hell happened?" Angela managed to pull herself up to a sitting position and rubbed her temples.

"I don't know. I saw you waving at me and I ran after you. But when you turned, it was someone else wearing the Hazel wig. That's all I remember. I don't know what to do. Any suggestions?"

"The good news is that my transmitter is still in my pocket. The bad news is that I doubt the signal will penetrate the rock around us. But maybe they can find us from where they lost the signal." With some difficulty, Angela pulled a keychain out of her pocket and pushed a little button. Mikela was delighted to see a tiny beam of light at the end of her friend's hand.

"Let's see what we've gotten ourselves into," Angela said as she scanned the area around them. "We can see about a foot directly in front of us with this little gadget, at least until the battery runs out. What do you say to some exploring?"

Mikela stood up and shivered. She reached a hand out to help Angela stand. "It wouldn't hurt my feelings any if we got some fresh air—and soon!" she said, trying to lighten their mood. She gave Mikela directions to hold onto her waist, rather than her hand, so they would walk as one, not side by side, hopefully lessening the danger of falling into a lower chamber.

Angela led the way very slowly, inching along, careful of every step, without any light but the one in her hand. She bumped into a pile of something rough and patted it with her hands, attempting to identify it. "There's a huge coil of chain in front of us, Mikela, I'm going to go around it." The women inched their way around, hugging the massive coil. "Do you hear something?"

The women stopped for a moment and both could hear a very low humming sound as well as the lapping of waves. Had they heard it all along or were they getting closer to the opening of the cave? As they rounded the coil of rope, Angela looked up. At least thirty feet above them, they could see stars in the midnight blue of the evening sky. A length of chain made of huge links led from the center of the massive coil up to the perfectly round hole in the cavern.

"Oh, no. It can't be..." Angela whispered. She stopped in her tracks and let go of the chain pile, turning around to scan the area behind her, eyes remaining upward. She stopped moving when she spotted the faint glow of a red light.

"What is it, Angela? What's wrong?" demanded Mikela. "Angela?! Answer me!" Angela just stood for a moment, trying to gather her thoughts.

"Bad news, Mikela." she hesitated before continuing, reaching out for the hand of her friend. "We're not in the caves." Angela sighed and bit her lower lip, fighting back tears. "We're not even near the caves. At the other end of this huge chain is an anchor...we're in the cargo hold of a freighter and if I'm right, we're anchored about ten miles away from the lighthouse." She heard the sharp intake of breathe as Mikela processed what she'd just been told.

Chapter Twenty-One

Angela and Mikela had flattened themselves as close to the metal wall as possible, ears alert for the sound of approaching footsteps, praying no one could hear the pounding of their hearts. It had been a long and slow journey from the belly of the ship, finding their way to the deck. After recovering from the initial shock of realizing where they were, the women decided they had two choices—either wait where they'd been deposited and hope for the best, or find their way out of the cargo area and up to the deck where they'd have a much better chance of Angela's transmitter signal being picked up by the F.B.I.'s tracking equipment. They had no idea how long it would be before they would be missed by their kidnappers. So far, they'd only seen two guards having a cigarette break outside the hatchway of the cargo hold. The armed guards were walking and talking, not noticing or looking for anything out of the ordinary. Although Mikela couldn't be certain they were speaking Arabic, she'd been around the world enough times to realize what she was hearing wasn't a European or Oriental language. The talking and footsteps gradually faded away, as did the pounding of her beating heart.

Angela crept out of the shadows and peered around the corner. In an instant she was gone. Mikela stood back, waiting for Angela's 'all clear' signal, surprised by the lack of crew members patrolling the deck. She filled her anxious moments with thoughts of Jim, wondering if he was safe, if he knew where she was, if she'd live to hold him again.

How long had Angela been gone? It seemed like an eternity ago that she woke up in the ship's belly and it had taken a lifetime to find all the right stairways and ladders to make it up on deck...please, God, don't let anything happen to Angela...her thoughts were running wild until she saw Angela's familiar outline slinking back into the shadows next to her.

"Okay, we have to go midway down the ship, slip over the side and into the launch. It's a rubber deal, with a small outboard motor and I'll bet it's what they used to bring us out here." Angela dug around in her pants pocket until she pulled out a makeup compact and handed it to Mikela. "Is this yours?" Mikela nodded. "Ok, then we know it was running not too long ago. There's a gas can in the back of the launch that felt pretty heavy, so I think we'll be able to make it back to the mainland. When we break for it, just follow me and don't look around. Don't hesitate. When we drop the lines that secure the boat, we need to try and hold onto the ropes to slow its fall. We'll be about ten or fifteen feet above the water. If you let the rope slip through your hands, the rope-burn will peel your skin off. We'd also drop and make a helluva splash, so we don't want to do that, either. We'll alternate each side until we're in the water and I'll start the sequence. Okay?" She rattled off instructions in a no nonsense chant, then reassuringly touched Mikela's arm. "Are you sure you're up to this?"

Mikela patted Angela's hand and nodded. "Let's do it."

"Okay, take a deep breath and follow me." Angela grabbed Mikela's hand and peered cautiously around the corner. No guards were at either end of the deck. "Okay, all clear. Let's go!" She took off at a sprint with Mikela close at her heels, pulling her along by her hand. The metal ladder that led to the launch seemed a mile away as they ran silently down the metal decking.

Mikela never once looked back and kept her eyes focused on the ladder's railing. Angela was up and over the railing in a split second and Mikela followed, somewhat awkwardly, behind her. She missed a rung on the ladder and hit her knee hard, but kept right on going. As she slid into the raft, Angela motioned her to go to the front.

Each end had heavy rope lines they would need to release. Mikela turned to see how Angela untied the knots and how she held it for the best leverage. She did her best imitation of the athletic woman's movements and soon nodded that she was ready for the release. Angela slowly let about two feet of rope ease out and her end of the launch tilted downward. Mikela did the same, holding on to the rope with all her might. Finally, with a loud slap, Mikela's side of the launch was on the water. They rubbed their arms for a moment getting the circulation back, and Mikela joined Angela by the outboard engine. Angela had removed the gas cap and stuck her finger in the tank to see if she could feel gas. The tip of her middle finger came up wet, so the tank was still pretty full. She breathed a sigh of relief as she screwed the gas cap back on.

The launch was floating alongside the freighter and Mikela looked up at the dark, massive wall of metal. It was frightening in the eerie moonlight. The longer they delayed, the more frightened Mikela became. Her knee was now throbbing and she feared that at any second someone would look over the ship's railing and spot their escape. Her heart was beating in her throat when at last, the motor roared into life. The launch seemed to hover for a second and then, with Angela at the rudder, the little boat made a half circle as she angled the craft away from the ship. They picked up speed, and as Angela got her bearings from the constellations, made another half circle, opened the throttle and smacked the waves hard in her effort to put distance between the launch and their captors.

Suddenly, a bright light from atop the ship's radio tower broke through the blackness of the night. They could hear a siren sounding an alarm over the roar of the launch's engine. Mikela looked back over her shoulder and could see men running to the railing, some shouldering rifles. Angela moved the rudder to the left and then to the right, trying to zig-zag the boat out of the range of the rifles. "Get down, Mikela!" Mikela felt something flit by her face and realized that the men were shooting at them. She tried to make herself a much smaller target within the boat and slid off the seat, onto the floor of the craft. Angela had tried to sit lower in the stern and as Mikela turned to look at her, saw Angela's arm jerk violently as a bullet found its mark.

Mikela scrambled over the seats to her friend. Angela winced in pain and held her right arm, blood seeping through her fingers. Mikela took over the rudder and kept weaving the boat, terror filling every second as she waited for another bullet to hit one of them. The launch finally passed through the farthest reaches of the spotlight's illumination and Mikela felt like they just might make it to the safety of the island. She didn't know how far they'd traveled, but in the distance she could make out the dark expanse of the island and even the red tower lights from the radio station.

Oh, thank you, God! They were going to make it! Angela grabbed onto Mikela and gasped, "Don't let up. Get us to the island as fast as you can. They hit the boat, so we need to get as close to shore as we can get before it sinks. I'm not gonna be able to swim."

Mikela used a sock as a makeshift tourniquet around the wound to help stop the bleeding. As Angela tried to find a more comfortable position, Mikela grabbed the rudder. Occasionally she looked back over her shoulder to see if they were being pursued, and was surprised to see nothing behind them. Even the spotlight had been extinguished. Maybe there weren't enough crew members on board to risk chasing the escaping captives? At any rate, she was grateful that no one was shooting at them now. The air was slowly escaping from the rounded sides of the rubber launch and in a moment or two, the craft would be swallowed up by the sea. Mikela had hoped to recover their purses, but she didn't dare leave the rudder to move closer to the front as her weight up there might cause them to sink even faster. As they got closer to the shore, she saw the welcome sight of her lighthouse. Even unlit, it was beautiful. She could see the sheer wall of the bluffs and the darker black shape in the side of the bluffs beneath the lighthouse, where the entrance to the caves was located. They would be able to climb up to the lighthouse the way she'd come down the first time...when she'd promised Jim she'd wait for him...

The little craft had started taking on water at an alarming rate. Angela tried to sit upright and was pleased to see how far Mikela had brought them towards shore. They only had a quarter mile or so of water to cross before they'd make the beach.

"Well, this is it, Angela. I'm just going to let the launch sink from underneath us. Can you float on your back? I'll finally get to use my lifeguard training and tow you to shore!" Mikela shouted, trying to sound confident, hoping that the distance wouldn't be more than she could handle.

As the motor sank lower into the ocean, it sputtered as it went down leaving a tiny whirlpool in its wake.

Mikela released her grip on the rudder as Angela lay back on the water. After a few tries, she used her good arm to help her tread water. Arching her back and treading with the good arm, she finally managed to stay afloat.

Mikela swam a few strokes toward her friend. "Are you all right?" she panted. Angela tried to smile as Mikela maneuvered her left arm under Angela's chin and began stroking the water with her stronger right arm. The water was ice cold as she tried to focus her concentration on the shoreline, rather than her throbbing knee and bleeding friend. Slowly but surely, the distance to the cave's entrance lessened and Mikela finally stood and touched bottom with her feet. She looked down at Angela and reassured her that they were almost at the lighthouse. She pulled Angela along until they were just a few feet from shore. Putting her friend's good arm over her shoulders, Mikela walked out the water and onto the beach. The two women collapsed on the sand, breathing hard and shivering from the chilly night air.

"Well, well, well...and what have we here?" Mikela felt a boot nudging at her side. She struggled to get to her feet.

"Oh, thank God! My friend's been shot and..." She stopped as she turned and looked into the cold, hard face of Ross Daniels. "No...Oh, no."

"And I suppose you'd like me to call 9-1-1 for you, wouldn't you, sweetheart?" Ross sneered. "I see you forgot to bring those fleabags with you tonight." Ross prodded her with the butt of the rifle he was carrying. "Get moving, Mikela. If your friend doesn't get her ass up in two seconds, she's dead." He aimed the rifle at Angela's head.

Mikela ran the few steps to her friend and helped Angela to her feet. "Where are you taking us, Ross?"

"Oh, I have a little surprise waiting for you, Mikela, something really special, because you're my special girl." His manner both frightened and angered her as she once again had Angela's good arm draped around her neck. "I'm going to take you on a little underground tour. We'll see just how much fun we can fit in before high tide. That's all the time you and your buddy have left."

At the foot of the cave's entrance, Mikela had to let Angela manage for herself as they climbed the six-foot gap between the beach and the floor of the entrance. Angela's face was contorted as she maneuvered her feet between the rocks, her bad arm dangling at her side. She finally fell onto the flat rock of the entrance and yelled in pain as she rolled onto the wound. Mikela rushed to Angela's side and helped her back to her feet. The two women walked silently into the blackness, tears streaking their cheeks. Ross kept taunting them with how many foreign men were waiting for their arrival inside the cave, just waiting for their first taste of American women, and how he was going to sit back and watch it all. Wouldn't that teach her a lesson in humility, maybe she wouldn't be so uppity in her next life. His psychotic cackling filled the air.

Mikela tried to think fast as they hobbled deeper into the cave. Ross was a raving lunatic, nothing he said made any sense. He was babbling and delusional. He kept smacking Mikela in-between her shoulders with the butt of the rifle and she was afraid that she'd topple on Angela as they were walking through the tidal pool area of the underground caverns. She heard the wail of the 'ghosts' as they got closer to being underneath the lighthouse. The tide still wasn't at its lowest.

There were lighted torches set every fifty feet or so into the rock walls of the caves and she kept glancing upward, looking for the ladder that would lead directly into the secret room in her lighthouse. The shadows were so dark, she couldn't be certain she'd ever find it and even if she did, Angela probably wouldn't be able to climb the ladder. She had to think of a plan to get them both out in one piece. Angela was getting weaker by the moment and would need medical attention soon. She lurched forward again as the rifle's butt smacked her hard in the back. Ross laughed hysterically as the women stumbled ahead.

Ahead, the main chamber of the cavern's maze glowed brightly from the intensity of the light inside. It looked as though they had stepped into a James Bond movie. There was a giant metal shark in a huge pool to the right of them. The ramp leading up to the 'shark' had a line of men pushing carts that held giant silver shell casings. Was it some kind of ammunition, Mikela wondered? They were loading thousands of these things into the submarine.

"Hey fellas, lookee here!" Ross shouted at the working men. "I brought dessert for tonight!" his laughter echoed through the rock chamber.

Mikela shuddered as she saw the hungry eyes staring back at her. All had jet black hair and swarthy complexions. That must have been the reason for the lack of crewmen on the ship—they were working here in the caves.

"Keep going, sweetheart," Ross said in a sing-song voice, as he smacked Mikela in the back again. They walked on past the submarine and line of carts, further into the enormous cavern. While Mikela was checking the right side of the massive chamber as they passed, Angela pretended to be in worse shape than she actually was and committed what she could see to memory. There were several tunnels leading off every hundred feet or so on both sides. Some were lit, while others were just dark doorways. Toward the back of the huge chamber sat a large rectangular building with clear windows and a wide stairway leading to its main door. The women could see several men looking down on them as Ross urged them up the stairs. Arriving at the top step, a man held open the door for them as they stumbled inside the building. The door closed behind them.

"Good morning, ladies," came a voice from the back of the room. A dapper looking gentleman in a military uniform came up to them and offered a seat on the only bench in the room. There were two separate desks, both housing radio equipment and computers that looked to be the command center of the operation. "I hope Mr. Daniels didn't inconvenience you too much. May I offer you some coffee?" He'd already begun pouring the strong beverage into three Styrofoam cups. "Sugar? Milk?" Mikela nodded "yes" to each and eagerly reached up for the cup he handed to her. Angela did the same, almost grateful for the warmth of the drink.

"It's unfortunate, Miss Williams, that you choose this particular time to claim your lighthouse. In another 48 hours, our mission would have been completed and you would never have stumbled upon our business. It's unfortunate for Miss Strongheart as well. We have cleverly concealed our operations underneath the lighthouse for many years. It was time for a change, but you 'jumped the gun' on us, so to speak and now I must make the decision of what to do with you both." Mikela inspected the man as he spoke. Probably in his late forties or early fifties. He had a muscular build and the ramrod-straight posture of a soldier. His hair was jet black, graying around the temples, complimented by his neatly trimmed salt and pepper mustache. He was mannerly and respectful, but his eyes were cold and dead.

"I know what to do with them," Ross leered. "I'm going to sell them to the highest bidder. I just thought you might like first refusal, General." Mikela and Angela huddled closer together on the bench, both holding their hot coffee, the only weapons at their disposal.

"Mr. Daniels, you disgust me. These women are going to die in a few hours, there will be no tales to tell. There's no need to torture them. Unless you would like to join them, I suggest that you leave us now."

"The hell with you! I found them, they belong to me." Ross growled. "Get up! Now!" he shouted to the two women. When neither one of them moved, Ross picked up the rifle, intending to strike.

Before Ross had a chance to swing the rifle, the General had his own handgun out of its holster and trained between Ross' eyes. "Take him away," commanded the General to the two other men in the room. "Put him with the other prisoner." Ross fought all the way down the steps, held firmly between the two guards. "I apologize for Mr. Daniels' behavior. But you know how these Americans are," the General chuckled at his little joke.

"Before you kill us, General, could you tell us what's been going on here? And what that ship is doing anchored off the island? I assume that's your vessel?" Angela asked, finally feeling safe enough to take a sip of the warm liquid. Imitating Angela, Mikela took a sip of her own. It smelled awful, but it went down pretty good.

"I'd be delighted. As you know, Agent Strongheart, I'm the military commander of Black Tide. My particular fascination in weaponry is biological warfare. Contrary to popular opinion, I'm not a cruel man. I don't believe in torture as so many others do. Land mines, bombs, weapons that only maim and do not kill hold no interest for me at all. Since no country in the world would offer me the testing facilities needed to launch a full scale biological global attack, I had to search the world to locate a facility of my own. I happened to meet Mr. Daniels through our website," the General took a sip of his coffee. Mikela stared in amazement as this man calmly sat and explained his plan to kill thousands of people in an attempt to control the world's fuel sources, as if they were having a neighborly chat. "Fascinating things, these computers." He stroked the nearest one on the desk he was leaning on. "Of course, it all boils down to money." The General shook his head. "And where else but America, is money a God? Your Mr. Daniels told me of a place that no one knew of, but himself."

"How did you learn to speak English so well?" interjected Mikela. "You speak better than most educated men in this country."

"Thank you, Miss Williams. Your own country took care of that for me. I was an exemplary student and came to the United States in my late teens. Your government paid for my western education. It's where I learned that power is in the hands of a few madmen. I plan on changing all that in the very near future." He set his empty cup down.

"To put it in the hands of a single madman?" Angela smiled sweetly.

"Agent Strongheart, call me chauvinistic, but I don't expect a woman to understand the workings of power." He gave Angela a patronizing smile. "Shortly after we leave our little hideaway, your friends in the F.B.I. will storm in and trigger the release of the spores that are contained in our silver canisters. The spores cause pulmonary/cardio function to cease. You, Miss Williams, Mr. Daniels and his prisoner, and your friends will all be killed by these same spores. No one will be able to venture near these caves for a hundred years, as the spores lie dormant until making contact with a dark and moist environment. Once they attach themselves to a host's lung tissue, it's just a matter of a few hours until death occurs. The canisters will be unloaded onto my ship and from there, every major airport and post office in the countries of my choice will be shut down within a matter of minutes. I won't bore you with all the details of distribution."

A loud beep followed by a string of foreign words, came from the radio across the room.

The General broke into a big smile that revealed two gold-capped teeth. "Well, ladies, if you'll follow me, I'll take you to Mr. Daniels and his friend now. My men are waiting for me." He very courteously allowed them to walk down the stairs as he picked up his briefcase from beside the door and, flicking off the light switch, followed them down the stairs.

"This way, please." He led them behind the office they'd just been in and motioned for them to enter into one of the lit passages. "If you'll follow the passage fifty more feet, you'll find Mr. Daniels and his companion. It's been a pleasure to meet you, ladies." He saluted them and turned on his heel, marching toward the submarine.

"Are you okay, Angela?" Mikela worried, looking fearfully at her friend's arm.

"I'm okay. It hurts like hell, but it went through my skin. Nothing's broken. Even the bleeding's let up. If we get out of this alive, though, don't you dare take me back to the hospital in Bangor!" Angela tried to make a joke to ease the tension they were both feeling. "Let's see where Ross is. If he hasn't simmered down, then we'll leave him here to fend for himself."

The women walked single-file, down the narrow passage. It opened into a room-size chamber, about the size of a small bedroom. There were two single cots in it. A torch lit the room, held in place in a niche on the wall of rock over the commode. The room smelled of salt water and human stench. On one cot, a man underneath a blood-soaked blanket made them catch their breath. On the other cot someone lay trembling beneath a filthy blanket. They went to the trembling blanket first and with her good hand, Angela gingerly lifted the blanket. Mikela did a double-take. The man lying on the cot was an emaciated, bearded version of Ross Daniels! "Oh, my gosh! Do you see what I see?" she asked Angela. One gray eye slowly opened and took in the two women looking down on him. "Oh, thank God," is all he said before bursting into tears.

In awkward silence the two women looked at each other in disbelief. It was hard to believe this skeleton of a man was still alive. He regained his composure after a few moments. "I'm sorry." Was all he said before struggling to sit upright. Mikela and Angela helped him to a sitting position and sat beside him on the little cot.

"Can you tell us who you are?" Angela gently asked. "My name is Angela and this is my friend, Mikela. How long have you been here?"

"M—my name is Ross Daniels," whispered the man. "I've been here for at least a year, maybe longer. I went to the Behavioral Center to pick up my twin brother, Luther, back in July. I brought him to my place so he could spend the summer with me. He quit taking his medication and one day decided that he didn't want me around anymore. He was going to take my life over. And I guess that's what he did." The real Ross Daniels choked on his own words and violently coughed for a few minutes. "I think I might have pneumonia."

Angela and Mikela looked at each other over Ross' head. "Ross, we're going to try and find our way out of here. Do you think you're strong enough to come with us?" Angela inquired.

"I can't leave Luther here, no matter what he did." Ross nodded his head toward the bloody blanket in the next cot. "I doubt I'll make it very far. I'm pretty weak. I haven't had much to eat or drink since I've been here." The little he had spoken seemed to wear him out.

"Mikela, could you help Ross out and I'll catch up with you in just a minute? Thanks." Mikela tried as gently as she could to help Ross stand and put his arm around her shoulder. She couldn't believe how little the man weighed. He wasn't any effort to carry. At least six feet tall, he couldn't have weighed more than a hundred pounds. He was reluctant to leave the room, but Mikela prodded him along in a soothing monotone.

"It's okay, Ross. Let Angela do her work, she's an F.B.I. agent. So is her brother, Jim. And I know he'll be here soon. Don't worry about a thing. We'll get you to a doctor right away and get some good food into you..." Mikela rambled on trying to ease Ross' fears as well as her own. She was worried about the General's remark that the F.B.I. would be here and trigger something to release the spores that would kill them all. She refused to die until she held Jim in her arms at least one more time!

She set Ross down on the steps of the General's office and told him wait there until she returned. She went back into the cell and came around the corner just as Angela replaced the blanket over Luther's face. "Are you okay, Angela?" Angela nodded her head, but it took a moment before she could speak. "It looks like they hit him in the face. It must have broken his nose badly enough for the bone fragments to penetrate his brain. The Ross we knew is deader than a doornail." Mikela put her arm around Angela and gave her a hug.

"It's okay, Angela. We're going to make it," Mikela smiled as she hugged Angela tighter.

"If my brother doesn't marry you and make you my sister when we get back to the real world, I'm gonna kill him, " Angela laughed and cried at the same time. They walked out of the chamber and back into the main room of the cavern. They heard strange sounding noises that rose and subsided as the submarine closed it's cargo hold 'jaws' and began to prepare to submerge. After a few moments, the 'shark' sank beneath the waters of the huge pool and the three wet, miserable and bloody survivors let out a simultaneous sigh of relief.

Chapter Twenty-Two

Once the submarine was safely gone, Angela stood up. "Time to radio headquarters where we're at so we can get ourselves rescued." She started up the steps, slowly putting one foot in front of the other, when out of the main passageway she heard the clamor of an approaching army. At least two dozen men, clad in black from head to toe, stormed the chamber, guns pointing at the three weary people on the steps of the office.

"F.B.I. Hands behind your heads. Step away from the stairs." Angela turned and stepped down, putting her one good hand behind her head. Mikela helped Ross to stand and they did the same. It was frightening to watch all those weapons being pointed at them, no matter whose side they were on. Angela looked over at Mikela and winked. Mikela smiled back and whispered to Ross not to worry. A white ball of fur bounded from behind the wall of black-suited men, heading straight for Mikela.

"Abby! Oh, Abby!" Mikela dropped immediately, despite the pain in her swollen knee and threw her arms around her furry friend. She buried her face in the fur and was the happiest she could remember in quite a long time. Where there was Abby, there would be Jim!

From out of the crowd of men, one came towards them. He pulled off his gas mask and handed it to Abby. Mikela looked into the smoldering dark eyes that she'd grown to love over the past few weeks and saw his concern for her. Niska trotted up to nudge her leg with his nose. She stroked Niska's head and ears as Jim helped her to stand and warmly wrapped his arms around her. He looked up, past Mikela's wild mane of hair, at a smiling Angela, Wilson by her side, as his sister gave him a 'thumb's up' with her good arm. "I told you I'd be back," he whispered in her ear. He picked her up in his arms, turned around, called to Niska and Abby and carried her out of cavern.

Jim, Mikela, Angela and Wilson stood at the mouth of the cave. The dogs made a graceful pair, leaping to the sandy beach below and having a romp in the waves.

"We can't leave until we know what'll happen to Ross Daniels. That poor guy is just about dead."

"Ross Daniels?" Jim exclaimed in surprise. "Where is he? It's payback time for what he's done to both of you." Angela and Mikela held Jim back and explained what Ross had told them about Luther. "Ross and I worked together a few years back and one day he disappeared. I figured he was working on another case until I knew what he did to Angela. I didn't even recognize him just now," Jim's anger subsided. "I remember he had a twin brother who was institutionalized."

As Jim was deciding whether to go back into the cavern, two black-clad agents came out carrying a makeshift gurney with Ross lying in it. They stopped at the gathering.

"Ross, how are you, buddy?" asked Jim. He took Ross' hand. "I was so happy to see Mikela and Angela in one piece I didn't even look at who was with them!" Ross looked up at Jim's face and smiled. Johnson and Hennessey came from the depths of the cavern and met up with the group. The two agents sheepishly hugged Angela and then Mikela, glad to be reunited. Jim spoke with Ross for a moment, trying to disguise the shock he felt at seeing his old friend so emaciated. But Ross' upbeat attitude gave Jim hope that he would, in time, recover.

"It's good to see you again, Jim. When I get a little meat on my bones, you'd better watch out. I'm going after both these ladies!" He managed another smile at Jim's stricken look. "I'm okay, just tired and weak right now. If I can get someone to feed me, I think I'll be all right. I don't think Luther will be that lucky."

The men carrying Ross laid the gurney on the stone floor of the cave's mouth. They climbed down to the sand and reached up as Jim and Wilson helped hand the gurney and its occupant down to them. They led the way to the sandy beach as Mikela and Angela followed. A helicopter had landed on the sand and the men loaded Ross onto the waiting Bangor Air-Evac, under Niska and Abby's supervision. Mikela stiffly climbed down the stones to the beach, and let Jim set her down on the sand. Wilson lifted Angela from her perch on the rocks and set her down beside Mikela and, arm-in-arm, the four walked to the Air-Evac unit. Angela and Mikela turned back and waved goodbye to Hennessey and Johnson and the two men who'd carried Ross out. Abby and Niska were already secured inside the helicopter, eagerly waiting for their master. As the four climbed on board and settled into their seats, they lifted off in a whirlwind of sand and water, bound for St. Joe's.

Chapter Twenty-Three

"And that's what happened," Mikela drained the last of her coffee and set her cup on the table. She looked up at Sophie, who was shaking her head in disbelief. She'd spent the last half hour with Sophie and Otis, bringing them up to date on what had transpired over the past week. In between their regular lunchtime customers, Mikela and Angela filled them in on their helicopter ride to the hospital and what had become of Ross and his twin brother, Luther. After the lunch hour rush was over, Sophie and Otis rejoined the women at one of the tables in the back of the store.

"That explains a lot, doesn't it?" Sophie refilled Mikela's cup. "Do you think Ross will be all right?" Sophie replaced the pot on the hot plate and sat back down at the table.

Mikela added milk and sugar and thoughtfully swirled the liquid around in her cup. "Yes, Jim told him back at the hospital. Even though he was sad about it, I think he was relieved as well. I guess he'd been taking care of Luther for years, visiting on all the holidays and bringing him home when he had vacations."

"Such a big responsibility for such a young man," Sophie sighed. "I always wondered why someone as nice and handsome as he is never married."

Otis shifted uncomfortably in his seat. "I feel downright awful that I didn't recognize the difference. Shoulda' known better."

Mikela patted Otis' arm. "No one knew, Otis. Even at the state trooper barracks they didn't have a clue and he's worked with those guys for how long? Eight or ten years? Don't be so hard on yourself," she tried to console him, but Otis kept his head down.

"Now look, you two. What Mikela didn't tell you is that we have a surprise coming here in a few minutes, so you need to put on your smiley faces!" Angela commanded. The older couple looked up at Angela as the screen door opened at the front of the store. They could hear the clicking toenails of Niska and Abby on the hardwood floors as they came down the aisle.

"Ooh, I'd better get my furry friends a treat!" smiled Sophie. "Otis saved them some beef bones from the butcher, so he can bribe them into staying with us," she laughed as she walked into the back room.

The dogs trotted up to the table, Abby heading first for Mikela, then to Angela for a pat and finally, both dogs were at Otis' side. "Just like having grandkids," Otis smiled, scratching behind the ears of both dogs. Sophie came from the back room and Niska and Abby ran up to her, each eagerly taking their bone. Everyone at the table looked up as Jim slowly appeared from around the middle aisle, his hand on a very skinny Ross' elbow, leading him to the table.

"Ross!" Sophie and Otis both sprang from their seats and went to their friend, plying him with dozens of questions, Sophie hugging him to her ample bosom several times.

"Wow!" Ross smiled, still in a weakened condition. "It sure is nice to be home. I've been craving your coffee for a long time, Sophie." Otis had pulled another chair to the table, while Sophie brought a mug and fresh coffee to set in front of their long-missing companion. She went to the pastry display and chose several of Ross' favorites, placing them on a plate and set those next to his coffee cup. She smiled down at him, voicing her concern over his dramatic weight loss.

"I think you'd best plan on staying here with us until you're feeling better," Otis said as he looked into the younger man's eyes. "You know Sophie won't rest 'til you put some meat back on your bones. We can make the couch up in the backroom into a bed, so you'll have your own room." Sophie stood behind Ross, rubbing his back and smiling, tears welling up in her eyes.

Jim joined the group, giving Mikela a peck on the cheek before sitting down between her and Angela. Mikela noticed his eyes darting toward the front of the store every few minutes. Sophie broke away from Ross long enough to bring a fresh pot of coffee to the table. She smiled down at everyone, in her element now, a mother hen with her chicks.

"Now I want all the details of what's happened since you all got out of there. Are those maniacs still running around under the island?" Otis demanded.

"No, they high-tailed it out of there," Jim recounted, "but they didn't get very far. We had Coast Guard and Navy craft circling the freighter and a nuclear sub on standby. We've got their mini-sub and crew in tow right now. Unfortunately, the General seems to have disappeared. We don't know how he got away or where he'll end up, but one thing's for sure—no reasonable country will give that madman a place to hang his hat." Jim patted Ross' shoulder and smiled. "But with this guy's help, I think Intelligence will be able get a fix on him. Ross spent a lot of time with the General and his men. He's picked up quite a bit of information that we otherwise wouldn't have had." The group chattered away, Jim still glancing toward the front of the store every few minutes. At last the screen door opened and Jim jumped up from his seat. "I'll be right back," he said, mostly to Mikela. He squeezed her hand and gave her a quick kiss, before heading toward the front of the store.

"I wonder what that's all about?" Mikela asked in surprise. Mikela saw Otis and Sophie smile at each other. She looked at Angela, who shared a conspiratorial giggle with Ross. "What!?" she demanded, looking in turn at each of her friends. Angela shrugged her shoulders in reply and kept smiling at Mikela.

"Abby! Niska! Bring Mikela!" Jim's voice came from the front the store. On that command, Abby and Niska dropped their bones where they were gnawing on them underneath the table and came over to Mikela. Abby reached up and took Mikela's left hand in her mouth, while Niska took her right hand. They started pulling her along toward the storefront. Mikela laughed and went with the dogs willingly.

"Will somebody please tell me what's going on?!" she giggled. The dogs paused as Wilson came toward them, and continued on down the aisle. "Wilson! What are you doing here? What are you guys up to?"

She followed as the dogs continued to pull her along. They stopped as they approached Jim, Mikela's eyes level with his belt.

"Hi, sweetie," Jim said. "Ok, Niska, Abby, let Mikela go."

The dogs released her hands and sat on their haunches. Mikela, still giggling, straightened up and wiped the dog slobbers on her jeans. As she looked up at Jim, she saw that he wasn't smiling, but looking rather nervous. He started to speak, then licked his lips. Abby gave a loud, "woof!" and Niska did the same. The dogs seemed to spur Jim into action. He brought his left hand from behind his back. Nestled in his palm was a tiny, black velvet box. "Honey, this is for you." Niska growled, got up and nudged Jim's leg. "Oh! Thanks, boy!" Jim got down on one knee as Mikela took the offered box from Jim's hand and opened it slowly, a thousand thoughts running wild through her mind.

"Oh, my gosh...." Mikela sighed. "Jim, it's gorgeous. Just beautiful...I, I..." she stammered as she took the ring from its box. Abby woofed again, twice this time.

"Mikela, I love you. Abby and Niska love you. Will you...will you marry me?" Without taking his eyes from hers, Jim took the ring from Mikela. He then picked up her left hand in his and slid the simple gold circle with the sparkling stone onto her finger. It was a perfect fit. "We really need you to complete our family." Mikela's eyes welled with happy tears, as an ear-to-ear smile broke out on her face.

"Oh, Jim...yes! Yes! Yes!" She took his face in her hands and kissed his lips a dozen times. As he rose from his kneeling position, a shriek echoed through the store. "What the...?" Mikela started to turn, but Jim held her close, and gave her the deepest, sweetest kiss. A kiss to seal their fate.

"It's okay, honey. Angela just got a surprise, too," Jim muttered through his kiss. After a few private moments, Jim and Mikela headed back to the tables, arms around each other. The dogs went back to their spots under the table, picked up their beef bones, and with their mission accomplished, got back to the business of some serious bone-gnawing.

"Well, Wilson? Was that scream a good one or a bad one?" chided Jim, punching his friend's arm. Mikela and Angela thrust their hands out at the same time, showing off their engagement rings to each other. Sophie "oohed" and "aahed," happy and excited for her friends.

"Well, this is just wonderful!" Sophie gushed. She was teary-eyed once again and walked over to Otis, who reached his arm around her.

"I hope you kids are as happy as we've been all these years!" Otis grinned. "You know, this woman let me chase her 'til she caught me!" he snorted in laughter.

The double-wedding took place during a magnificent sunset on the bluff side of the lighthouse. Mikela and Angela made beautiful brides as they walked arm in arm to stand beside the two handsome, tuxedoed men awaiting them. A justice of the peace stood with his back to the ocean as the two couples swore solemn vows to each other, promising a lifetime of love and commitment. Completing the intimate wedding party was Ross, who served as best man, with Niska and Abby as ring bearers and a doting Sophie and Otis as witnesses. As Jim and Wilson stood facing their brides, the justice of the peace pronounced the two couples 'husband and wife.' Jim didn't wait to hear the words "you may kiss the bride" as he bent over his beautiful Mikela's face, his lips seeking hers, her wild mane of hair encircling them both. The happy onlookers applauded in approval, welcoming a beaming Jim and Mikela Strongheart and Anthony and Angela Wilson into their midst. Niska and Abby joined in with happy and excited barking and prancing, as the red-orange remains of the fading sun slipped slowly underneath the black tide.

The End

Printed in the United States
36951LVS00004B/4-72